Freya stared at Kjell as he disappeared into the white froth twisting and turning before her in gusts of wind that pulled at her hair and her clothes. Stuck? Here?

No!

For how long? What would she do? Where would she—

She shook her head, trying to lessen the cascade of questions falling on top of each other. She had meetings back at the palace. *Oh, God.* Her fingers pressed against her lips in shock.

The dull beat of fear joined her pulse as she hurried forward, her steps difficult and ungainly from where the snow hit her at her calves. Everything in her wanted to call to Kjell, but she wouldn't. She could just make out the prints his shoes had made in the snow and had enough sense to follow them to the cabin. She was panting by the time she reached the wooden steps up to the front door, sweat awkward and slick on her back, sticking her base layers to her skin. She pushed open the door, expecting to find the cabin empty, but Kjell was standing there with his back to her.

"I can't stay here."

Pippa Roscoe

SNOWBOUND WITH HIS
FORBIDDEN PRINCESS

HARLEQUIN
PRESENTS

Recycling programs
for this product may
not exist in your area.

ISBN-13: 978-1-335-56952-3

Snowbound with His Forbidden Princess

Copyright © 2022 by Pippa Roscoe

For questions and comments about the quality of this book,
please contact us at CustomerService@Harlequin.com.

Harlequin Enterprises ULC
22 Adelaide St. West, 41st Floor
Toronto, Ontario M5H 4E3, Canada
www.Harlequin.com

Printed in U.S.A.

Pippa Roscoe lives in Norfolk near her family and makes daily promises to herself that this is the day she'll leave the computer to take a long walk in the countryside. She can't remember a time when she wasn't dreaming about handsome heroes and innocent heroines. Totally her mother's fault, of course—she gave Pippa her first romance to read at the age of seven! She is inconceivably happy that she gets to share those daydreams with you all. Follow her on Twitter, @pipparoscoe.

Books by Pippa Roscoe

Harlequin Presents

Virgin Princess's Marriage Debt
Demanding His Billion-Dollar Heir
Rumors Behind the Greek's Wedding
Playing the Billionaire's Game

Once Upon a Temptation

Taming the Big Bad Billionaire

The Diamond Inheritance

Terms of Their Costa Rican Temptation
From One Night to Desert Queen
The Greek Secret She Carries

Visit the Author Profile page
at Harlequin.com for more titles.

For my editor, Hannah, who lets me get away with more than I probably should be allowed to, and who always makes my books better.

My thanks are unending. (As is my penchant for a trilogy.) xx

CHAPTER ONE

'YOUR HIGHNESS? HIS MAJESTY will be with you in a few minutes.'

Princess Freya of Svardia nodded, resisting the urge to press her palm against the erratic pulse of her heart. She reminded herself that it was her brother who would take this meeting, not her father, who had—as Svardian tradition held—stepped down from the throne at the age of sixty-five, as his father had done and his father before him. The tradition ensured that whoever graced the throne was mentally and physically strong, whilst also reflective of the broadest generations of Svardia's subjects.

The reigning King—her brother Aleksander—would mark his first year while their father and mother left on a twelve-month sabbatical, away from the country and out of contact to ensure no risk of interference or influence while both the new King and the Svardian people got used to each other.

Three months ago, Aleksander had ascended the throne. And now, hands clasped firmly behind her back, she stood outside his office and prepared to go to battle with her King.

A bird soared past the window, catching Freya's eye and taking it over the spring green garden that extended all the way to the walls separating the palace from Svardia's capital city of Torfarn. It was a view she'd seen a million times but never given real thought to. Now, though, it had become uniquely precious to her.

The simple beauty of the ancient trees, the subtle delicacy of the hornbeam hedges used in the sixteenth-century maze, the neatly manicured lawns and the sprawling natural park just beyond, each was a piece of evidence left by the successive generations of one of the world's oldest royal families. Her heart pounded a single dull thud as she wondered what Aleksander, her brother, would leave behind for his future generations.

Perhaps after she stepped down from her royal title, she could get a job showing tourists around the palace. The laugh that should have followed the ironic thought got caught in her chest and she closed her eyes.

She loved doing what she did. Being who she was. The sense of history, the grandeur, the respect for tradition and the symbolism of it all.

And most of all she loved having the ability to use her position and title to support the causes and people that needed it, ones that sometimes the people of Svardia and their politicians forgot. But she also knew that the responsibility of being royal was a duty that few could understand. And even now she felt a sharp sting at the cruel irony that meant she could only do her duty by *not* doing her duty.

The door behind her opened and two palace staff passed into the corridor, their conversation quietening and their heads bowing as they saw her. She waited, facing the door, able to see glimpses of the room her brother had taken as his office. It didn't matter how much modern technology Aleksander filled it with, his office—just like every other room in the palace—was inescapably *grand*. The preservation of the baroque style that filled the Rilderdal Palace had been a matter of pride for her father and a source of embarrassment for her brother.

'Freya? Get in here, I don't have much time.'

'You know,' she said, stepping into the room and closing the door behind her, 'you really should get a secretary. You can't just go about shouting at people from your office.'

'Didn't you hear? I'm King. I can do what I like.' Freya honestly couldn't tell whether the statement was pure arrogance or a dark notion from his new role, now that their parents were on their sabbatical. Not that it mattered. His statement hadn't required an answer.

Once, it might have been different. When they had been younger, *he'd* been different. But around his seventeenth birthday Aleksander had changed. The soft warmth that she'd shared with him gone in the blink of an eye with no explanation whatsoever. And in its place? A controlled and forbidding man who was closed even to her. Now she could rarely tell what he was thinking, let alone planning. In that moment, Freya wondered at the price they had both paid for the throne.

'Are you sure that this is what you want?' he asked as his gaze assessed her face for a reaction. She stared blankly into irises that were so dark they were almost black. Hers were the opposite—the palest amber—and their younger sister Marit's a perfect meld of the two, a startling hazel.

Freya could have laughed at his attempt to catch her out, so she might reveal that it was the last thing she wanted on this earth. But she'd been trained well—such a perfect princess that even in this she was the better diplomat than he.

'Yes. My mind is made up.'

Aleksander grunted an unintelligible reply

and turned to look out of the window, framed by the much-detested pink curtain. 'What do you think Father would say?' he asked, his tone surprisingly solicitous.

Her stomach turned. She knew what their father would say. That she was doing the right thing—the only thing that could be done. But saying that would make her brother more likely to dig his heels in, so instead she stalled. 'We won't know for another eight months until their return.'

'You could contact them. If you wish?'

Freya wondered why he believed that would make any difference at all. Their parents wouldn't thank her, instead seeing it as a concern only for the King of Svardia to handle. And if she expected emotional support, well… Freya, Aleksander and Marit each knew better than that.

'I don't think that he'd appreciate the break with protocol.'

'Even for this?' he pressed.

'This is *my* problem. I've always known how important the line of succession is.'

'If you give me time—'

'Aleksander,' she interrupted. 'If anything were to happen to you before you have children, or to your family in the future, the line of succession falls to me and…' She clenched her jaw, still struggling to vocalise it.

'Ifs,' Sander replied.

'Ifs that happened to our father!' Freya frantically tried to call back the emotion in her voice. Having had to take the throne after the shocking loss of his older brother, her father had always made sure she knew how important she was as the second child. And she had borne the weight and responsibility of that duty, and would have continued to do so until her dying breath. Even after discovering that she could not fulfil the full extent of that duty.

'Marit is going to struggle.'

'Yes,' Freya agreed. 'But I will help her in any way I can.'

Her brother snorted out a frustrated breath. 'Of course you would help your replacement, no matter how much it costs you.'

'It is my duty. And she's our sister,' she replied simply.

'She's going to have to marry. And soon. And Freya—the same rules will now apply to her. She will have to marry a noble, just as you would have had to.'

Freya could only nod. She hated that Marit had been dragged into this. Hated not only the archaic legislation that determined the man she would marry, but also hated just how much her younger sister would struggle with the constraints of her new duties. Freya had been born knowing her duty, knowing the restrictions it placed on her life. But Marit had always been the wild one, and she and Aleksander had indulged her, enjoying her freedom even if they couldn't have it for themselves.

'I'm sorry,' she said, the words thick and heavy on her tongue.

'It's not your fault. And I'm still not convinced it's necessary.'

'Really? It's three months since your coronation. If the press find out about me when you are still unmarried and without—' Both her heart and mind stumbled over the word.

Children.

It whispered and screamed in the silence between her and Aleksander. Behind her back, she clenched her fists, warding off the visceral ache that swirled in spaces that would never be filled.

'Freya—'

She put up a hand to stop him. 'If the press find out, Aleksander, it would be carnage.' She could see it so clearly. The press would rip apart any dignity or privacy that she had. Across the globe, doctors, celebrities and everyday Svardians would be asked for their opinions on the failure of her body. 'But the backlash wouldn't just be on me, Aleksander. They would dig into your life, Marit's… And you are already under such incredible scrutiny–'

'Freya…' he warned.

'Aleksander, I believe in you. I believe in what you are trying to achieve for Svardia. But there are already whispers that you are too progressive, and too fast with your changes.'

'And that is my duty to bear, not yours.'

'And mine is to make sure that nothing disrupts what you are hoping to accomplish.'

'They will tear you apart, Freya.'

'Yes, they will,' she replied, not naïve about the backlash that would ensue. 'But not because of my failure as a woman. We will tell them that I have chosen to step down in order to spend time working on myself. We all know how much the press love to hate a self-involved royal. It should keep them busy for quite some time.'

And, that way, it would at least appear as if it were her choice. That way, she might be able to fool herself that she had managed to preserve her agency by controlling the narrative. That way, she might protect her dignity. Her *identity*.

Because to have her femininity questioned, her womanhood… Her heart shook, cowering from the threat of such a blow. She would lose *herself*. So, no. She couldn't face that. Better to let them think her selfish and uncaring of the institution into which she had been born and loved with her every breath.

'If I had children—'

'But you don't,' she said simply.

'But I *will*,' he bit out through clenched teeth, as if it were something that would cost him greatly. But her curiosity over it wasn't enough to distract her from the argument they'd been having for the last month.

'Yes, but in how long? Two or three years' time? No palace can keep a secret for that long. The news of my infertility will get out in the next three months, maybe? Six if we're lucky. If I step down, my fertility won't even be a question and we have a much greater chance of keeping it quiet for the length of time you need.' The possibility that the media would never discover her infertility was only a distant hope for Freya.

'You have an answer for everything.'

'Because I have thought about it every which way.' And Freya had. Her heart ached unbearably. She would never have willingly stepped away from her family, from her role. But if it meant securing the stability and future of her family and country, then her decision was simple.

'Well, then I have one last duty for you to

perform, Your Highness,' he said, going to stand behind his desk, no longer her brother but her King. 'I have a Medal of Valour that needs to be delivered to its recipient.'

Freya frowned. 'I don't understand. Medals are received at the investitures.'

'The recipient refuses to attend the Investiture.'

The Medal of Valour was offered to military personnel who had demonstrated exceptional courage in the face of extreme danger. But to refuse it from your King—the Commander in Chief—was not only unheard of but would reflect badly on Aleksander, especially at his first Investiture. It would be seen as a vote of no confidence, no matter what reasons were behind the refusal, and that could be a devastating blow to Aleksander's rule.

'Why would they not want the medal?'

'That is for you to find out when you take it to him.'

Him. Her brother wasn't usually so coy with his words. She stared at him, just as able to play the royal waiting game as he.

Aleksander sighed. 'Kjell Bergqvist.'

Fire and ice swept in waves across her skin and her heart stuttered, forcing Freya to stifle the gasp of breath her lungs cried out for.

'No.' The word shot from her lips unbidden.

'This is not up for debate.' His voice was quiet but his eyes sparked gold and his tone was implacable. 'If you want to step down from your duties, your title and your family, then by God don't expect me to make it easy for you.'

'Sander—'

'The helicopter will be here in an hour. Be on it, or not.'

Her brother was no longer looking at her, peering down at a piece of paperwork in the same manner their father always had when he couldn't be bothered to utter a dismissal.

No choice. No choice. No choice.

'An hour?' she asked, hating the weakness in her voice.

'I believe there are weather constraints,' he replied, still not looking up.

Freya shot a glance to the window, frowning at clear blue skies.

The helicopter jerked suddenly, Freya's stomach lifting into her throat as she battled a swift wave of nausea, but no one in the small cabin would have known it. She had spent years perfecting serenity in the mirror and she wore it like a crown. The pilot righted the helicopter, apologising into the earpiece of her headphones, and she sent him a smile of reassurance.

Usually, she loved watching the ground roll out beneath her as the helicopter sped through the air, but all she could see was shifting shades of white as they crossed from Svardian airspace into Swedish.

'Who is this guy anyway?' she heard the young guardsman whisper to Gunnar, the head of her royal protection detail. Freya couldn't help it, she turned to find Gunnar's eyes locked onto her and she felt the burn of a blush rise to her cheeks. She turned back to the window and forced her gaze back to the shifting white shapes beyond.

'Lieutenant Colonel Bergqvist is a highly respected and valued member of the Svardia Armén,' Freya heard Gunnar explain behind her.

Lieutenant Colonel?

She tensed to prevent her body from betraying her reaction, trying to figure out how the tall, lean student she'd once known could have become such a powerful soldier. But then, she thought, turning back to the white static outside the small window, she hadn't actually known anything about him at all.

She gave into the hazy memory she hadn't revisited for eight years…

She'd been in a helicopter just like this one, shaking not from turbulence but from shock.

What made it so awful was that it wasn't just a reaction to the terrifying news that her sister had been in an accident and was being treated urgently by Svardia's best doctors. No. It was the horror that had come from realising that her boyfriend, the person who had made her laugh, made her feel safe, wanted and desired, the man she had given her kisses to, *herself* to, had been an undercover bodyguard, hired by her father.

He sat opposite her in the helicopter that was returning them from Switzerland to Svardia, staring at her as if she were an unexploded bomb. She clenched her jaw as her heart twisted, and turned away to look out of the window so that the three Close Protection Officers couldn't see the tear that had rolled down her face.

Four. There were four CPOs with her in the helicopter.

Less than forty minutes earlier she and Kjell had been in her dorm room, laughing. Freya couldn't remember what about now. It had taken her months to make him smile, and the first time he'd laughed she'd felt it deep in her heart. They'd been laughing, but it had petered out to a moment when happiness had settled and desire had stirred and he'd been about to kiss her...just like he had done a hundred or so times in the last few months.

She craved his kisses with a ferocity that overwhelmed her.

His phone had rung and something had passed across his eyes at the strange ringtone she'd not heard before. Three seconds later her phone had rung too. It had been her brother, telling her that Marit had been in an accident and they needed her to come home immediately. Fear had slashed through her. Her heartbeat had raced and concern had become a powerful white noise that blocked out everything but the ringing in her ears.

Kjell had looked up and seen the horror on her face, placed a hand on her arm to anchor her. And it had worked. He'd calmed the storm and soothed her pulse enough to hear what Sander had said next.

'Marit's going to be okay, Freya. She is. But we need you here. We have a Close Protection Officer nearby who's going to come to you. We can argue about it later, but now he's going to bring you home. His name is Bergqvist. Kjell Bergqvist.'

Her stomach had roiled, filling her with nausea and horror.

She'd begged her father not to give her a protection detail. She'd wanted so much to prove to him that she could be trusted. That she would be a perfect dutiful princess during her time at the Swiss university. She'd meant every word of it.

Until she'd met Kjell.

Humiliation scoured her stomach. Not only had she proved herself to be anything but the perfect princess—she'd done it with the very man who had been sent to spy on her.

The man now sitting opposite her in the helicopter.

A tear rolled down her cheek. For the months of their secret relationship she'd fought it—the knowledge that it could never be. That neither her father nor the legislation that bound the royal family would allow her to marry a commoner. But in spite of that she'd wanted him. She'd taken a risk for him. She'd fallen for him because he'd made her feel loved for who she was, not what.

Freya battled the sob rising in her chest because the one thing that had become more precious to her than any other was based on a lie. And how could you love a lie?

She tensed her body to keep it from betraying the shivers that racked her heart. The betrayal she felt was like a bell being struck over and over again in the deepest part of her heart,

*vibrating outwards and causing her whole
body to tremble.*

'Freya.'

His voice made her clamp her eyes shut tighter.

*'Bergqvist,' came the warning response from
the senior CPO.*

*It was clear that while none of them knew
anything specific, her reaction to the revela-
tion of his identity had been extreme.*

*Humiliation painted her cheeks bright red. If
they didn't know, they must suspect that something had happened between them.*

'Freya,' he tried again.

*When she ignored him, he ripped off the
headset and released the belt holding him in
place. He reached across the distance between
them and took her face in his hands.*

'Bergqvist!'

'We need to talk about this.'

*'There's nothing to talk about,' she whispered
harshly, trying to wrench herself from his hold.*

Oh, God. It hurt so much.

'I wanted to tell you so many times.'

*'Back in your seat, Bergqvist—that's an
order!'*

*He stared at her, his eyes full of need and
yearning, and all she saw was betrayal.*

'It was real for me,' he said.

She tried to shake her head, but his warm hands held her firm.

'It was real for me,' he insisted.

She stared him deep in the eyes, the pain in her heart like nothing she'd ever felt before. She thought she heard it break.

'I never want to see you again.'

In shock, he released her, and she turned to look out of the window.

For the entire flight back to Svardia she didn't once take her gaze from the small plastic circle.

She waited for all the men to file out of the cabin before she moved, and when she did she kept her gaze on the floor until she could look ahead without even catching so much as a glimpse of him.

She cut him from her life and her heart that day, swearing never to think of him again.

'Your Highness? We're coming in to land,' she was warned through the earpiece in the headphones, jolting her back from a memory that left a fresh bruise on her heart.

The pilot put them down much closer to the edge of the forest than Freya had thought possible. Yet it was still a good distance from the two dwellings she could barely make out, buried beneath what looked, worryingly, like several feet of snow.

She waited while green jump-suited men flipped buttons and muttered into their headsets, controlling her breathing by timing her pulse to the slowing blades above her.

'Okay, Your Highness. We're ready.'

She nodded to Gunnar and reached up to the handle just above the open door. The young member of the royal guard, eyes bright and cheeks flushed with excitement, held his hand out to her from the ground. This was probably his first assignment. Had she been Kjell's first assignment too?

'Your Highness?'

She turned back to look at Gunnar.

'We don't have much time. Conditions have worsened unexpectedly. There's a storm coming in from the East and it's set to be a bad one.'

Freya didn't waste any more time. There was absolutely no way that she would risk getting stuck out here. None. She had one goal. Get in, have Kjell accept the medal and leave. He owed her that much at least.

She landed a little ungracefully, despite the support from the guard, the blanket of snow about three inches deeper than she had imagined. The action jarred, sending a hard jolt up through her body. She shook her head a little, righting herself and her sense of self at the same time.

This was what she wanted, she told herself firmly. This was what was needed.

Freya looked up at the large cabin closest to them, the red painted wooden boards barely visible through flakes of snow that were now falling thick and fast. But something drew her gaze to the cabin set further back, nearer the woods, and a sense of déjà vu struck her, even though she'd never set foot in this part of southern Sweden before.

She shivered as a snowflake snuck past the upturned collar of her coat and slid down her spine. The icy tendril clashed with the fast burn of ire, flaring to life at the mere thought of what could have been and what would never be, the past with Kjell and the future with children she'd never have all swirling out of her reach and making her heart ache.

Her head snapped up as she felt his eyes on her, burning her skin. She searched back and forth across the front of the properties and only on her second pass did she see him leaning lazily against the corner of the furthest building, watching them approach as if he had all the time in the world.

Pinpricks broke out across the back of her neck and a shocking longing hit her hard and fast. It stuck in her throat and filled her lungs. Until the memory of his betrayal cut through the haze of need like a shard of ice.

Clearing her mind, Freya knew without a doubt that the only reason she had spotted him was because he'd allowed it. And now that she *had* seen him she refused to look away, half afraid that if she blinked he would disappear and all of this would have been for nothing. Her only chance at freedom gone, just like that.

The snow made it much harder to close the distance and consequently gave her more time to take him in. How was he standing there in the middle of a blizzard with a minus wind-chill factor in nothing but a dark long-sleeved top that clung to his torso like a second skin? The matching trousers looked military grade and even had she not overheard his army rank she still would have thought *dangerous*. He was twisting something in gloveless hands—a rag or piece of cloth? Her fingers stung at just the thought of how cold his hands must be.

Finer details began to emerge as she drew closer. His hair, still the colour of spun gold, had grown a little long at the top, was swept back by the wind but the close crop at the sides highlighted the fierce slash of his cheekbones. The dark material of his T-shirt pulled tightly

over a chest that was bigger and broader and
so much more defined than she remembered
it made her palms itch. The narrow circumfer-
ence of his hips was marked by a thick black
canvas belt that looked utilitarian rather than
affectation. And his height... She could have
hurt herself looking up at the forbidding ex-
pression on his features.

Maybe it was the snow, maybe it was the iso-
lated cabins, but she'd expected a beard. Full,
thick, something a Norse god could be proud
of. But his jaw was clean, all hard angles and
smooth skin, and still she wanted to—

Freya jerked her eyes up to his and bit her
lip. The storm in his gaze was far worse than
anything the elements could throw at her. He
narrowed his eyes as if sensing her wayward
thoughts, before he refocused on something behind her.

'Take her home, Gunnar,' he growled, his
voice somehow carrying through the raging
snowstorm, and without even a second glance
at her he disappeared through the door with a
slam that dislodged an unhealthy amount of
snow from the sloped roof.

Panic shot through her. It had taken two
months for Sander to even consider agreeing
to her request to step down from her royal position. If Kjell didn't accept the medal, would

her brother force her to endure the world's press poring over her failure as a royal? As a woman?

The thought of it gave her the fuel she needed. She clenched her jaw, turning back to the head of her security, sending her arm out to stop him. 'Don't even think about it,' she warned, barely seeing him raise his hands in surrender before she marched towards the cabin and the closed door.

'Fifteen minutes, Your Highness. Twenty at most,' she heard Gunnar call to her as she reached the cabin.

CHAPTER TWO

WHAT WAS SHE doing here?

Kjell stood in the boot room, his hands on his hips and his eyes on the middle distance. It was only when his teeth started to hurt that he realised he'd been clenching his jaw. He tilted his head to one side; the wind was picking up even more speed outside and when it hit, the storm was going to hit hard, but it was the crunch of snow he was listening for.

He'd heard the helo above the *thunk* of his axe cleaving through the last pieces of firewood he was stockpiling ahead of the storm. The sweat he'd worked up instantly cooling on his skin, making the hairs stand up on the back of his neck.

He'd watched as the pilot navigated a decent proximity to the forest with the resigned determination of a military man who knew something grim was coming. But he hadn't expected *her*.

For a moment, his mind had blanked with a

shock he didn't think he'd felt since he'd last seen her. His response to her twisting and morphing back to the present through layers of anger, shame, guilt and heat. Always heat.

He clenched his jaw. He couldn't afford to think like that. Her Royal Highness Princess Freya of Svardia was outside his cabin and, no matter what had happened, he was a Lieutenant Colonel in the Svardia Armén. She was his superior, as a citizen and as a serving member of the armed forces.

She always had been.

Kjell figured he had about twenty seconds before she reached the door, with a possible three-second margin given the worsening conditions. He knew that his order to Gunnar would have frustrated a royal who'd experienced years of people bowing and scraping. But even as that thought registered, he knew it was wrong. Freya had never been like that. At least she hadn't been eight years ago.

A thread of shame unspooled in his gut. Yes, he'd made a mistake back then. But she hadn't been faultless—and the memory of that sparked anger and resentment through muscles already corded with tension. A tension that, in the last few months, had been far too close to the surface. Now it rose and rose, too much and too quickly.

A slice of light exploded like a flashbang across his thoughts and suddenly he was sweating, an infernal dry heat drawing moisture from his body as surely as it had done from the dry clay earth. He squinted, dazed, into the midday sun, surrounded by shouts and screams, a child crying, thick smoke in the air, and blood…

His heart missed a beat and he forced a deep inhalation of air into his body, holding it still for six seconds, and slowly exhaled. He did it again, until his heartbeat was back under control and the icy fingers of a cold sweat retreated from his skin.

The crunch of snow outside grounded him.

It didn't matter why she was here, he'd find that out soon enough. He just needed to be ready. Dragging his senses back under control just as he heard the creak of the wooden step outside the cabin, he turned to face the door, squaring his shoulders and steeling himself.

A moment later the door was pushed open and she was standing there, looking nothing like the girl he remembered.

It was her laugh. That was what caught his attention, despite the fact that he was sitting at the back of the lecture theatre. Even without it, he would have known where she was. After all, he'd followed her that morning from her dorm all the way to the humanities building.

But the sound of her laugh as one of the other female students whispered something to her cut through the chatter of the other hundred and twenty-nine students, excluding the three who were missing that morning with Freshers' Week hangovers. He had helped compile reports on every single one of them and he knew more about these students than their own families.

Shaking off the strange sensation the sound had caused, he rubbed his chest, blew out a breath and bounced the rubber end of his pencil on his notepad. He shouldn't be here. He should be back in Svardia, completing his officer training assignments.

He'd wanted to be a soldier for about as long as he'd known his father had been in the army. Brynjar Bergqvist had been an Överste in the Swedish army, but had given it up when he moved to Svardia after marrying Kjell's mother.

While his typically quiet father had never said, Kjell understood how much he missed it and why, despite being offered a position in the Svardian Armén, his father had politely declined. Brynjar's heart might have belonged to his Svardian wife, but his allegiance was to Sweden and its King.

Kjell had hoped that his being in the army might bring him closer to his stern, taciturn father, but he'd never know. Because he was shadowing some princess studying political science. He clenched his teeth, imagining his father's reprimand at the frustrated bent of his thoughts.

She is not just some princess. She is the figurehead of your country and she is owed your loyalty and your duty.

Kjell straightened in his seat and scanned the audience as the lecturer entered the hall. Two points of entry and exit. The bank of narrow rectangular windows high up across the back wall had no line of sight, and he was four rows back and across from the Princess and could get to her in under three seconds.

Of course, Kjell's job would be much easier if his hands weren't tied by his having to be undercover. But the King had decided that he would prefer to give her the illusion of freedom—which required a CPO she had not seen before. So he had been pulled out of the army, having just passed basic with flying colours, and given six months' intense training in close protection, then sent off to university in Switzerland to guard a princess with hair like molten chocolate and eyes that were hauntingly pale, like clear amber.

He felt his jaw tense again and purposefully relaxed it. During the prep for this position he'd watched every single bit of footage he could find, explored every part of her life on paper and online. In short, he'd done everything that someone looking to harm or leverage the Princess's life would do.

What he'd gleaned was that Freya was an eighteen-year-old who led a very structured life. Although she had been heavily involved in royal duties from the age of fourteen, her school records indicated an excellence born of hard work as much as inherent intellect. Her extra-curricular activities were focused on helping others and she had absolutely no trace of scandal anywhere.

Unlike some of her European counterparts, Princess Freya seemed to have found genuine happiness in her title, as if she had been made to fit her role completely. Always perfect, always calm, and strangely open in a way that lessened people's natural inclination to cynicism. As such, Kjell had fully expected to be bored out of his mind.

But nothing had prepared him for the impact of her in real life. Because while he'd surveyed her from the corner of his eye, watched her openly, stayed within two feet of her in the corridors, hallways and walkways of the uni-

versity, she'd never once looked at him. Until this moment in the lecture theatre, when she leaned her head back, frowning just slightly as if looking for someone, and her eyes rested on his and caught them.

In that exact moment a crack formed in the tight leash he kept on his control. A fine hairline fracture of his armour that was barely noticeable. Like a stress fracture. But if it was struck repeatedly the damage would be irrevocable.

A cold blast of icy wind slapped him in the face, snapping him out of the memory and plunging him back into the present.

'Close the door,' he ordered, his voice harsh to his own ears, as he turned to toe off his damp boots. 'You're letting out warmth.'

He'd needed the excuse to look away, but it had been too late. In a second he'd taken in everything about her, the after-image still bright against his closed eyes.

She was still utterly beautiful. Freya wasn't pale like some pampered European royalty. No, her skin was earthy, warm, and everything he'd ever wanted to sink into. Her eyes, hauntingly pale but bright and quick and…staring at him with hell fire.

A fur hat, the colour of espresso and dusted

heavily with snowflakes, made her eyes look almost feline. They had always been utterly unique, a shade of brown so light it was haunting. The press, both local and international, had obsessively compared them to those of a fox.

Beneath the hat, long streams of rich mahogany-coloured hair would be swept up and bound against her head. It was a style she seemed to have adopted after the night of her sister's accident which, thankfully, hadn't been as serious as originally thought. Above a long elegant neck was a jawline that led to a chin you wanted to hold between your thumb and finger. Mainly to angle a face so beautiful it made you search it for flaws. But he'd looked for hours and never found a single one.

No, he thought. The flaws, the coldness that had shocked him had laid deep beneath the surface. As if that remembrance brought out the critic, he found her a little thinner, more angular, less…soft. The thought was so intense he'd almost sounded it on his tongue.

'Pardon?'

'What?' he asked, surprised by her question.

'You said something.'

'No,' he denied flatly, despite wondering if it were a lie. If he kept his words simple, she might leave sooner. He checked his watch. From the sound of the wind outside, they had maybe ten minutes before the storm struck. And no matter why she was here now, he was one hundred per cent sure that she wouldn't be in nine minutes' time. She couldn't be.

'Aren't you going to say anything?' she demanded, as if flustered by his silence.

'*You* came *here*, Princess,' he growled, unable to keep the animal in him at bay.

'Don't call me that.'

Her tone was defensive rather than angry and it wasn't what he'd expected. It piqued an interest he really didn't want to have *piqued*. So he shrugged off her complaint and focused on what was pertinent.

'Why are you here?'

'Can we go inside?' She looked around the small boot room separating the cabin's front and internal doors, not with superiority that might have been expected from a royal, but rather as if she were uncomfortable.

He nearly laughed, aware that he must be miles removed from the polite courtiers that surrounded her on a daily basis. No, he was far from civilised. He was a soldier, forged in some of the world's worst hellholes on his missions seconded to the UN. He wouldn't diminish himself for her comfort. Instead of replying to her question, he shook his head. He had no interest in letting her any further into his cabin.

A faint flush rose to her cheeks as she cast her eye around the space, the old butler's sink behind him and the bench that had become a shoe rack beneath the coats and layers hung up by the door. It looked more rough than rustic. Inside, the cabin was anything but, though he had no intention of her ever getting that far. Yet there was an irony to it, he supposed. After all, she'd been the one to teach him that looks could be deceiving.

'I need you to accept the medal.'

A burst of white noise exploded in his ears, levelling out on a high-pitched ringing that left him a little disorientated. Then came a wave of outrage that washed away his patience. Fury tightened his chest. He'd told his commander he couldn't accept it. He'd even told the King directly. And he'd sent *her* here?

Kjell turned away and shut his mouth before he could curse, disguising his reaction by placing the rag in his hand on the shelf behind him. He breathed in and out through his nose, regaining composure, if not calm, before turning back to where she stood in front of the door.

'I informed command that I would not accept the medal.'

'I am not leaving here unless you do,' she warned, her tone making him combative. But it was there in her eyes, a flash that caught his attention. A desperation that didn't fit.

'Why is this so important to you?' he asked, following his gut.

'It will reflect badly on my brother if you do not.'

'No. It's not that,' he said, wanting to move, wanting to assess, to circle her like prey that had shown its weakness. Freya's words had been too smooth, too quick.

'It is all you need to know.'

The response cut him like a knife. Four months ago, it would have been enough. He would have stood to attention, saluted and done as ordered with a *Sir, yes, sir.* He would never in a million years have questioned a commanding officer, let alone his country's Princess or his King, no matter what had happened between them personally. Even now he wrestled with the need to obey, the legacy of his service and duty as one of the most respected and trusted soldiers of the Svardia Armén.

'That is no longer good enough for me, Your Highness,' he said through gritted teeth.

His tone, his words, they all said so much and so little. What had happened to him? Freya searched his face, his body, needing something, *anything*, to help her understand the change in him. This close up, she could see now, he was so very different. He stood with his arms crossed over his chest, emphasising the bulk of his biceps and the tense corded muscle along his forearm. Proud, determined, immovable. It was the kind of look that quelled rebellions and marshalled armies. She saw it then. The warrior that he'd become, the power that he wore like armour and hated that she found it magnificent.

She'd once told Kjell her fears, her hopes… her secrets. But to this man? No. This man was completely different. Maybe if she hadn't been so hurt, maybe if they'd spoken afterwards, maybe if they'd somehow made sense of the mess her father had caused when he'd sent Kjell to her undercover, she might have been able to tell him the true reason she was here. But she just couldn't trust him with that. Not any more.

He stared down at her, bright blue eyes shining with an intensity that threatened to strip away the layers of protection she had put in place. She had to get out of this cabin. And it had nothing to do with the fast-approaching storm and everything to do with him and what he made her think of. What he made her want. She hated it, the desperation she felt, the fear that had brought her here, to him. The tears that pressed against the backs of her eyes were hot and she blinked rapidly to try to keep them at bay.

'Kjell,' she said. His name so familiar on her tongue. Her body's instinctive softening around it like a muscle memory that hurt her heart. 'Please,' she said, hating the way that her voice nearly broke. 'I need this.'

But when she looked up at him the fierce anger in his eyes shocked her.

'You need this? *You*?' he demanded, his voice increasing in volume. 'You come here in a helicopter, demanding that I accept a medal like it's a favour to you after *eight* years during which I've not been able to go *home*?'

Freya stepped back instinctively to protect herself from the barrage of words flying at her. He'd not been able to go home?

'Kjell, I—'

He took a long stride towards her and she stepped back again. His eyes bored into hers as if she were the devil and he the righteous warrior. Another step forward, and one step back had her against the door of the cabin. She hated that he was using his body against her when that same body had brought her so much pleasure in the past. For a shocking moment she thought he wasn't going to stop. Wasn't sure she even wanted him to, and the blush that rose on her cheeks when he stopped as if reading her thoughts was one of pure humiliation. That was the feeling he always made her circle back round to. Embarrassment. He had played her for a fool once. She knew it, *he* knew it. Thank God no one else did.

'I don't know what you're talking about,' she said, trying desperately not to raise her hands between them to ward him off or reach for him, she didn't know. Flustered, she tried to hold onto the thread of conversation. 'Why haven't you been able to come back home?' she asked, unable to mask the quiver in her voice.

His eyes were an arctic blaze, flaring and sparking, his jaw clenched, the powerful neck muscles bunched as if every single millimetre of his entire body was tensed and ready to fight, but completely and utterly restrained.

He would never strike her, never ever cause her physical harm. She knew that with a certainty that she had about very little in her life at that moment. But it didn't mean he wasn't a threat. The emotional vortex he was pulling her into was something she'd avoided for eight years.

Her pulse leapt at the heat of his breath on her lips and she pressed her thighs together, trying to relieve the intense pull she felt between her legs. No one had ever affected her like this, no one other than him. She'd not even been this close to a man in the time since she'd last seen him. The smell of him was tauntingly familiar and making her ache in ways that she'd thought she'd forgotten.

'You said you never wanted to see me again.'

Her throat ached, as if she had only just yelled the words at him. They had haunted her for months after that night.

'Yes. I did.'

'Those words were clear enough to my commanding officer.'

'Your what? I don't know—'

'Tell me, Freya, what made you think that they would all ignore such an order from their royal?'

She looked up at him, still without any idea what he was talking about. What order? Her heart had been breaking over his betrayal. The young student she had studied with, laughed with, danced with, drunk with and slowly and gently given her heart to, given *herself* to…why would she *ever* want to see him again when she found out that he'd been employed by her father as her bodyguard? She didn't understand what he was trying to—

'Exile, Freya. You exiled me.'

The beep of the satellite phone's ringtone cut through her shocked silence and he didn't know whether to laugh or rage. That she hadn't even realised what she'd been doing all those years ago was incomprehensibly cruel.

'Answer it,' he said, disgusted with her, with himself. He just wanted her gone. He turned his back on her and walked towards the internal door to the cabin. He nearly laughed at the irony that *he* now wanted out of the very space he'd enclosed them both in.

No matter how much he wanted to walk into his sanctuary, he would not do it while she was still here. But he was at the very end of his patience. Her brother had taken this too far in sending Freya to deliver the medal, but he'd overplayed his hand. This refusal would be his last. He would *never* accept that medal.

He heard Freya speak quietly into the phone, unable to resist glancing to the side where he could just make out her turning away from him in his peripheral vision. The words grew urgent and louder, until, 'No, wait! Gunnar!' she shouted, flinging open his front door and disappearing into a flurry of blinding snowflakes.

Kjell cursed loudly and violently, grabbing his coat before shoving the front door closed behind him as he ran after her. He threw an arm into a coat sleeve as he jogged in the direction of the helo and strained to hear Freya's angry shouts in the distance as he pushed into the other sleeve. His heart pounded even as his quick mind began to process the reality of this new situation.

The blades were already in motion and he hurried forward, knowing that in Freya's state of mind the danger they posed might not actually stop her. By the time he caught up with her the helicopter was already two feet off the ground and the downwash was fierce enough to have her shielding her eyes. Her hat had fallen off somewhere in the snow and her long dark hair was streaming out in waves, buffeted by the air from both the helicopter's blades and the storm that was now, for all intents and purposes, here.

He pulled her back from the downwash, their hunched forms blindly retreating until they were far out of reach from the pounding waves of air and snow. From a position of safety, they watched as the helicopter jerked up into the air, hovering momentarily as if offering its regret for leaving her behind, before gliding up and away from view.

Kjell watched her as she stared into the sky long after distance and visibility had made it impossible to see, as if she couldn't believe that it wouldn't come back. He peered at the cabin through bloated fluffy flakes of snow that looked harmless until they overloaded a helicopter's engine, making it too dangerous to fly, or too dangerous to wait for the very important person they had left behind.

'Give me the sat phone,' he ordered.

She held it out to him without looking, her fingers already red from the cold. She couldn't stay here. She wouldn't last five minutes. She was too soft for his world.

He pressed the button as he turned back and headed to the outbuilding. 'Gunnar,' he shouted into the phone past the howling wind, 'I can get her out to the other side of the lake.'

'It's too late.'

'Don't give me that. Your pilot has done far more in worse conditions,' he said, noticing that Freya had started to follow him more quickly as she realised that he was trying to get them to come back.

'Not with a royal on board, Kjell.'

'That's bull and you know it, Gunnar.' Freya reached for the phone but he lifted his elbow out of the way and turned so she couldn't reach it. 'What aren't you telling me?' Kjell demanded, trying to keep his question out of Freya's hearing.

'I have my orders, Kjell. We'll be back to pick her up when the storm clears.'

Gunnar disconnected the call his end, leaving Kjell standing halfway between his cabin and the outbuilding where he housed his snowmobile, seriously considering just jumping on and getting as far away from Her Royal Highness Princess Freya of Svardia as possible.

'Well?' she asked, the flush on her cheeks and hope in her eyes brighter than the north star.

He took one last longing look at the out-building.

'Sorry, Princess,' he said without the faintest trace of sympathy. Stalking back to the cabin, he threw his next words over his shoulder. 'Looks like you're stuck here.'

CHAPTER THREE

FREYA STARED AT him as he disappeared into the white froth twisting and turning before her in gusts of wind that pulled at her hair and her clothes. Stuck? Here?

No!

For how long? What would she do? Where would she—

She shook her head, trying to lessen the cascade of questions falling on top of each other. She had meetings back at the palace. *Oh, God.* Fingers pressed against lips in shock. She was due to meet Stellan Stormare in three days' time. It was an appointment she could not miss. She looked back up to where she should have been able to see the cabins, but they were gone, hidden deep within the maelstrom of the storm.

The dull beat of fear joined her pulse as she hurried forward, her steps difficult and ungainly from where the snow hit her at her calves. Everything in her wanted to call to Kjell, but she wouldn't. She could just make out the punches his shoes had made in the snow and had enough sense to follow them to the cabin. She was panting by the time she reached the wooden steps up to the front door, sweat awkward and slick on her back, sticking her base layers to her skin. She pushed open the door, expecting to find the cabin empty, but Kjell was standing there with his back to her and—

'I can't stay here.'

She hadn't meant it to be the first thing she said. She knew how it sounded. Pampered and spoiled and demanding. But that wasn't why the words had rushed out of her mouth the moment she had caught sight of him.

He'd taken off his T-shirt for a reason Freya simply couldn't fathom and was standing there with his fingers on the top button of his trousers. He cast her a look over his shoulder, but she didn't catch it because she was too busy running her eyes over his back, the corded muscles and dips and...and scars.

'Don't look at me like that, unless you intend to do something about it.'

Distracted by the blatant sensual challenge, her head snapped up, her gaze clashing with the arctic fire in his. Anger, yes, a taunt, absolutely, but there was something else hidden beneath the boldness.

She looked away. She didn't have any more right to his secrets than he did hers. She doubted he would respect the retreat but she didn't know the rules with him. This wasn't the Kjell she had once known, who would tease her reasoning and thoughts out gently, with kindness and encouragement. This was a hard, unrelenting challenge and attack from a man with no reason for patience and she was owed no kindness.

He had been exiled? For eight years?

She opened her mouth to speak, but his words struck out like bullets.

'Boots off. Clothes off.'

She squeaked in shock. 'No.'

'Wet kills around here, Princess. If your clothing is wet, it's not coming into the cabin.'

'You can't be serious,' she exclaimed, looking for a joke, or the hint of one.

He simply levelled her with that glacial gaze. 'You might want to turn around.'

She felt distinctly as if the cold was affecting her brain function. Why would she want to—

The moment his hands went to his hips she spun on her heel, squeezing her eyes shut. Not that it stopped the images exploding to life on the backs of her eyelids. In her mind's eye she saw the full length of his naked body as she heard the slide of material against his skin and falling to the floor. Heat stung her cheeks as she imagined him plunging one leg and then the other into the dry pair of trousers she'd seen on the shelf unit by the door.

'You can look now, Princess.'

'Stop calling me that,' she said through clenched teeth. She waited an extra beat before turning around to find him looking at her with too much in his eyes.

'Boots off, clothes off,' he repeated tonelessly. He unhooked a white cord at the side of the room and lowered an old wooden slatted clothes pulley. He shook out his trousers and hung them up as she watched, eyes wide. He hadn't been joking. 'Hang your clothes here, there are dry ones there,' he said, pointing to the shelf. 'Boots go there.' He indicated the bench where shoes and boots were piled next to some strange spiked contraptions. Kjell cast one last look at her and disappeared through the connecting doorway.

Freya shivered despite the intense warmth of the boot room, clenching her jaw so that her teeth didn't chatter. Instinctively, she knew weakness wouldn't be tolerated by this man and she felt a wave of sympathy for anyone under his command. With red fingers that felt twice their normal size, she struggled with the laces on her boots. The sweat that had stuck her clothes to her skin now felt cold and clammy and she was beginning to see the benefit in shedding the layers.

He'd not been home in eight years, her conscience prodded. The thought of not seeing Marit or Aleksander for that long was inconceivable. But Kjell was an only child. No child should be cut off from their parents. Even if that child was a six-foot three-inch man with muscles that could have been sculpted by Michelangelo and a scowl that was, cruelly, more sensual than his charm.

She'd done that to him. She'd kept him from coming home.

No, she defended. She'd had every right to be angry, every right to be hurt when she'd found out the truth about him. Kjell had lied to her about who he was and had insinuated his way into her life… Her conscience yanked hard. Knowing that hurt was rewriting their history. In fact, he'd been reluctant to talk to her at the beginning.

'Is this seat taken?' she asked, her heart in her mouth.

Freya had never before been so bold. She'd never really had the opportunity at the all-girls boarding school she'd attended in Svardia.

Ice-blue eyes stared up at her blankly. She

*was about to turn away, utterly devastated,
when he said, 'No.' It was clipped and rough,
as if he hadn't spoken in a while, and had a
strange effect on her pulse.*

*She sat down with a sigh of relief. But now
that she was there, she didn't know what to
do next. She opened her mouth to speak, but
stopped when he got up, gathered all his books
and left the table.*

*She clenched her jaw until the blush of hu-
miliation had passed and promised never to
speak to Kjell Bergqvist again.*

Snapped out of the memory by a distant slam
from deep inside the cabin, she pulled the boots
from her feet and self-consciously stripped off
her clothes. But if he thought she was taking off
her underwear, he was sorely mistaken.

'Bra and knickers,' came the shout, as if he'd
somehow divined her defiance.

'Absolutely not!' she yelled back.

'If I don't see them hanging up on that dryer,
you're not coming in.'

'You're a beast!'

'You're not the first woman to say so!' he
shouted back without missing a beat.

Cheeks flaming and an unwanted but completely uncontrollable jealousy raging within
her, she peeled down her panties and unclipped

her bra. She refused to hang them up on the dryer though, like some trophy for him. Turning to the shelf of clothes by the door, she pulled out a pair of grey jogging bottoms, a white vest and a petrol-blue jumper that was surprisingly soft. As she put them on, the dry warmth that enveloped her reminded her of what it had felt like to be surrounded by Kjell, *protected* by him. What they'd shared eight years ago had been too intense for peace, too frantic for stillness, too risky to be safe. But she had found a serenity with him that she'd never experienced before. Which had made his betrayal so much worse. Freya used that hurt, that pain then, adding them to the layers of armour she would need. Because that was what being in his presence felt like. Going to war.

Kjell was prepared to admit he might have taken it too far, demanding Freya remove her underwear, but he'd needed to make a point. They were stuck here at the beginning of one of the worst storms he could remember in Dalarna, and if she didn't follow the rules there would be severe consequences for them both.

The cabin was state-of-the-art—not that she'd seen evidence of it yet—but it was still off-grid. The solar panels would be out of action from the snowfall in the next few hours, but the backup generator was ready to kick in. The ground source heat pump would be good for another day or two of ambient temperature but, even then, they'd have to rely on the wood-burner in the central part of the cabin. It was nothing he wasn't prepared for and there was enough food and water to last them both an entire month—not that it would come to that. The storm was bad, but would probably blow itself out within the week. Not that it made it any less dangerous.

To someone used to central heating, constant electricity and heat whenever and wherever they wanted it, the minus temperatures that this storm could reach would be shocking. All that kept them safe from the elements were the walls of this cabin, the ability to create heat and stay dry. If any of those were compromised, they would be in very real life-threatening trouble.

No matter what had passed between them, a threat to Freya was anathema to him. She was his to protect until the storm lifted. Something thick and heavy shifted in his chest. As if the thought was too much. Too close to what he'd once been.

Freya wobbled on heels that she was clearly unaccustomed to and that made Kjell even an-

grier. Her so-called friend had stayed on at the half-term party, letting Freya walk back to her dorm alone, in the dark, inebriated.

Kjell was tempted to have the girl transferred.

In the past two weeks alone he'd redirected the interests of one student determined to 'bag a princess', and another who'd wanted to cash in on her fame.

Princess Freya had the self-preservation instincts of a duckling.

She leaned a little to the left and he caught up with her just in time to balance her.

'Are you drunk?' he demanded.

Freya shook her head. 'Absolute not.'

He cursed.

'Why do you swear in Swedish?'

'You know Swedish swearwords?' he asked, surprised.

She nodded. 'And Greek, English, German, Italian and several in Russian,' she said proudly.

'Svardian tax dollars at work, ladies and gentlemen.'

'No. That's for my degree. I learned swearing on my own time.'

He had to bite back a smile. Beneath the layers of royal etiquette she was funny.

'Okay, Princess, let's get you home.'

He pulled her against his side, but she twisted gracefully in his arms so that they were chest to chest. She craned her neck to look up at him.

'So small,' she whispered.

'I am not small,' he replied.

'No... But I am,' she said, shaking her head.

His lips curved and her gaze flickered between his mouth and his eyes, her own wide and full of glitter.

'What?' he asked.

'You smiled.'

'I didn't,' he said, scowling.

'You did. I saw it. You can smile, Kjell,' she accused him, as if it was something he kept from the world.

The memory was a punch to the gut, more powerful for its sweetness. A possessiveness he'd never known before had filled him that day, one that had carried through until the very end. But even then it had just been an illusion. The Princess and the commoner? No. She could never have been truly his. He'd only borrowed her for a short time. And it had cost him greatly.

He had shamed himself and his parents by having a relationship with Freya, by lying to her and failing utterly in his duty. He'd accepted exile as his punishment, accepted that he deserved it. But that didn't mean it hadn't cost him, hadn't hurt him when he looked at his mother's teary eyes and met his father's distant gaze when he met them on the few hours each year he'd return to check in with Command. Didn't mean that he hadn't struggled to find his place in a different world.

The door to the cabin opened, the noise wrenching him back to the present, and he turned to find her face frozen in a look of surprise. Rosebud lips that had been ready to continue their shouting match dropped into the perfect 'O' as she took in the cabin that he'd poured years and savings into making perfect.

He'd just about calmed his breathing when he caught sight of her underwear in her loosened grip. Molten lava poured through his veins in a thick, slow crawl, lulling him into complete arousal that demanded appeasement. She'd been the only woman to ever have that effect on him. And he'd never tried to replicate it with another.

'It's beautiful,' she exclaimed, utterly unaware of the precarious position she was in. He tracked her progression through the cabin, jaw clenched and muscles tense. He wouldn't last an hour with her if he didn't get himself under control. *Now.*

Focusing his mind on the alterations he'd made to the cabin that had been in his father's family for generations, the mental exercise calmed him. Bare feet padded up to the window that wrapped around the entire length of the broad single-storey cabin. The feat of engineering had cost him four whole years' pay, but it was worth every single cent. As evidenced by the hypnotising effect it had on Freya. Unable to resist, he went to stand beside her, trying to see the panoramic view as she did for the first time.

'You did all this?' she asked, her hand reaching up to touch the triple-glazed reinforced glass created specifically to withstand the drastically cold temperatures that hit this central part of Sweden for nearly six months of the year, whilst simultaneously adjusting to the intense heat of the summer months.

He nodded. He felt her eyes on him but he locked his gaze on the most breathtaking view he'd ever seen. And he'd travelled the world. Even between the swirls of snow, the expanse of the view was startling. The large lake beyond was a smooth disc of grey ice, framed either side by the close press of trees that wrapped around to the front of the cabin, giving a sense of privacy, exclusivity, reinforced by the knowledge that no one else resided within twenty kilometres of these two cabins. The spindly evergreens blanketed by thick fingers of snow looked mystical and faintly threatening—black twisting into white, throwing off grey and disappearing into haunting shadows.

But to be protected by the glass and witness the ferocity of the wind hurling huge banks of flakes back and forth across the landscape, the sheer movement of it, while standing in what felt like the eye of that raging storm…that was the real pleasure, the real awe.

She turned to him, a smile on her lips and a spark in her eyes as if she'd forgotten herself for a moment, and that was when he saw her. The girl he'd once known. And then *he* nearly forgot. All the reasons why he couldn't just sweep her up in his arms to soothe the need that was choking in its intensity. Her title, his lie and the gulf between them that would never be breached. He'd nearly forgotten. But not quite.

As if reading those thoughts in his eyes, she turned away to take in the rest of the living area. In the corner, flames flickered in the wood burner warming the space easily. A large caramel leather sofa ran the length of the wall, covered in different types of fur throws, ones that his grandfather and great-grandfather had made themselves from the animals that had died naturally on the property. The Bergqvists had strong views towards living with and within their habitat. No animal was killed needlessly and no resource was used mindlessly or completely. Every change Kjell had made to the cabin had the highest environmental certifications and the latest technological advances. The cabin was as ecologically sustainable as humanly possible.

It was more than a cabin, though. It was his sanctuary. But as Freya crossed the threshold to his bedroom it felt like a cage. Having her here, invading his space, it made him feel too much. Mentally he paced the room, feeling trapped by her presence. He had come here to face what had happened on secondment four months ago. Not the woman who had exiled him eight years ago.

Freya stared at one of the biggest beds she'd ever seen. It was less a bed and more a raised floor area. Low to the ground, the mattress took up two-thirds of the room. There were no side tables or lamps, but as the room had the same window as the living area she presumed that the natural light would be sufficient. She was drawn once again to the view that made the cabin feel part of the landscape in a fundamental way. It was simply incredible, and somehow so Kjell. As if it perfectly captured the duality of the man—raw wildness and controlled restraint.

She looked back at the bed and suddenly realised what had brought her to the room. Frowning, she peered through the door to where Kjell was moving about the kitchen. A kitchen that was on the other side of the cabin. A cabin with no second floor.

'Kjell?' She saw his shoulders tense. She ground her teeth together, realisation making her heart thud. 'Where's the other bedroom?'

He turned, glared at her over his shoulder and, having clearly decided that she could answer her own question, he went back to whatever he was doing on the stove.

Oh, no. No, no, no, no.

She ran to the table where she'd seen her sat phone and jabbed at the keypad with shaking fingers. *Answer...please answer*, she prayed. Maybe Henna, her lady-in-waiting, could do something to get her out of here.

'Freya?' an urgent voice demanded when the call connected.

'Henna!' she cried, so relieved to hear her friend's voice.

'Are you okay? I was told about them having to leave you...where... Okay?'

'Henna? Are you there?'

'Can't...you,' came the panicked response.

She sent a look to where Kjell was leaning back against the sideboard, holding his coffee mug to his chest and observing her distress with a passivity that bordered on cruel.

'Kjell?'

He scowled. 'It's a satellite phone, Freya. It needs to be visible to the satellite. And while I'm sure your model has indoor capabilities, there is deep cloud cover and snow has piled up on the roof.' He stalked to where she stood by the table and took the phone from her. 'Henna, if you can hear me, she's fine. Check in with Gunnar Sydow for her return ETA.' He disconnected the call and threw the phone onto the sofa, before disappearing into the bedroom and kicking the door shut behind him.

Freya was at her wits' end. Nothing about today had gone as planned, from the meeting with her brother to this moment. She was stuck here with a man she'd never wanted to see again. Not only that but he clearly blamed her for something that had happened as the result of one sentence; one heartbroken, devastated cry of a young woman who'd had the most wonderful love ripped away before her very eyes.

'I didn't ask for this, you know,' she shouted at him through the closed door, when what she really wanted to say was that she hadn't wanted him exiled. She'd just known that she'd never see him again. She'd known, even then, eight years ago, on that helicopter ride as he'd begged her to look at him, to let him explain...she couldn't allow him to. Because what she'd felt for him all those years ago had been too much. Too strong. She would never have been able to let him go, even though she'd known that she wouldn't have been allowed to keep him.

The door was yanked open and Kjell emerged, his arms full of bedding, his face a blank mask. He stalked to where the sofas were and threw the bedding down.

The, *'It's all yours, Your Highness,'* was a growl between his lips as he passed her, heading back to the kitchen, and it made her want to cry. She sucked in a shaking breath, keeping it as inaudible as possible and slipped into his bedroom, closing the door behind her. She sank down with her back against the door, pressing a fist to her mouth.

All she'd wanted was to stand down on her own terms, without the press finding out, so that she could lick her wounds in private. The moment the doctors had told her that she'd never be able to carry a child to term, that the lining of her uterus was too thin for implantation, she'd known how the press would react.

They'd question her role—what use was a royal who couldn't produce heirs? And then they'd question Aleksander. Marit. And that was unbearable.

She was under no illusions, never had been. Her father had always ensured that the family did what was best for the country. It came first. Always. But he'd been especially hard on her. Perhaps because he saw himself in her. Before his brother's tragic death, her father had been second in line to the throne. Perhaps the shock, the weight of that responsibility, having to take that on while he should have been allowed to grieve had changed something fundamental in him. But it was as if he'd never seen her for *herself.* Only her ability to support Aleksander. Support the throne.

And she knew that when her father heard the news of her infertility his first thought would be that she wouldn't be able to do her duty. He would hurt for her, she knew that, but only after they'd protected the throne.

And it wouldn't matter what good she'd achieved as ambassador to her charities, as CEO to a women's science initiative, it wouldn't matter how skilled she was at smoothing ruffled diplomatic feathers. She would be known by absence for ever, by what she didn't have.

A working womb. The chance for motherhood. Children.

She'd never, *never* thought there would be a problem. That there was something defective, broken inside her. And she hated that her infertility made her feel less. Less hopeful, less free, less of a woman. But it was more than that, she realised as she pressed her back against the bedroom door. She felt it deep within her, constant, unconditional, infinite: all the love she had to give, but no one to give it to. Absent parents, a distant brother and a self-involved sister. And, her heart shuddered, a man she couldn't share it with and the children she'd not be able to have.

Her hand shook. She saw them so clearly, the little boy and little girl, each with blond hair and arctic blue eyes. *Kjell's.* She was shocked to realise that she'd never given up that dream.

A tear rolled down her cheek and she pushed it away, only another came and then another as she stifled the sound of her cries. But she clenched her teeth, determination filling her. No matter what happened, she couldn't let Kjell know why she needed him to accept the medal. Because he had been and would be the only person who had ever seen her whole rather than broken.

Kjell paced the kitchen area, not liking how quiet Freya was. She'd always had a poise about her, regal, something contained and restrained. But she had closed the door behind her over three hours ago and not opened it since.

Dark had descended and she hadn't turned on the light in the room. He'd have been able to see it through the crack beneath the door. An hour and a half ago he'd knocked to tell her that there was dinner on the table if she wanted it, but there'd been no response.

The caged animal growled that it was her own fault. But his conscience jabbed him in the gut, his stomach twisting with guilt. He'd behaved like the beast she'd accused him of being. His tone, words, actions towards her harsh and unforgiving. He could admit to that. He'd make it up to her, he promised her deep in his soul. But not before he got to the bottom of why she needed him to accept the medal. Because there was one thing he knew for sure. It had nothing to do with him or her brother and absolutely everything to do with her.

CHAPTER FOUR

FREYA WOKE FEELING absolutely awful. Her eyes were puffy and swollen and her throat sore, as if she'd swallowed sand.

Water. She needed water.

But that meant she'd have to leave the bedroom. And Kjell was outside. She closed her eyes. Kjell. There was just so much...*too* much. But she couldn't hide in here for the next however many days, no matter how much she wanted to. Last night, the hurt and pain had risen because she'd been shocked and exhausted. But she'd had her moment of weakness and now she needed to face reality.

Being stuck in Kjell's cabin gave her the opportunity to get exactly what she wanted. Him to accept the medal. And that wouldn't happen if she stayed hiding in his bedroom. Sitting up, she was struck by the stunning view from the windows. Unlike the sitting room, which was covered in pale blond wood, rich deep ochre-coloured leather and all the warm brown tones in between, Kjell's room matched the snowscape.

In the sitting room she'd felt cocooned and safe, protected from the outside world. Here, in his room, she was *part* of it. White linen, impossibly soft grey fur throws and wood flooring so dark it looked like charcoal. The wooden wall panels in here had been painted white but sanded back so that they blended with the wood's natural colouring. Even his clothes seemed to eschew colour as if he sought to camouflage himself in the winter wonderland.

As if thinking of him had worked some spell, her eyes snagged on movement out by the lake. Alert in an instant, she watched his figure move at speed across the edge of the frozen disc of water and into the woods. The misty breath streaming from his mouth spoke of a minus temperature that made Freya shiver. He was wearing a hat, gloves and layers enough to bulk out the torso she'd seen yesterday.

Heat, delicious, wicked and instantaneous, blanketed her at the sheer memory of him. Her woman's mind wondered how different it would be to make love to that man, but her younger self lashed out, still hurt and betrayed from years before, self-protection an almost violent need. Steeling herself, she threw back the cov-

ers and focused on showering before he could
return. The temptation to raid the kitchen and
grab everything she might need for the day was
fierce, but she was done hiding. At least she
would be clean, dressed and have her defences
in place by the time they went for round two.

The freezing cold air burned his throat with
every inhalation, but he forced himself on.
He was no way near working off the intense
need racking his body. All night long he'd had
dreams of Freya, born from the past, tainted by
the present. He was no stranger to frustration
and was more than capable of handling it himself. But it was different now that she was in
his cabin. Before, he'd been able to tell himself
he'd imagined how perfect her skin was, how
his skin felt on fire when she looked at him,
that the heat of her body made his heart feel as
if it were clawing out of his chest to get to her.

'Please don't,' she begged him, turning away.
*'Don't what?' he asked, pulling her back to
him, needing to see what hurt she was trying
to hide.*
*'Look at me like you want to kiss me when
you clearly don't.'*
*Everything in him turned to stone. He
couldn't move, because if he did it would be*

*to give her the one thing she clearly wanted...
and the one thing he had no right to give.*

*A blush rose to her cheeks under his gaze
and, before he could react, she rose on her tiptoes and pressed her lips against his.*

*For all their softness, they struck him with
the weight of an anvil. Shockwaves rippled out
over his body, down his legs, to his toes and
into the floor.*

*But when he still didn't move Freya pulled
back and looked up at him with such hurt that
it blasted the final brick in his determination
to stay away from his charge.*

*She went to pull back, but instead he drew
her to him, his lips found hers and his heart
found home.*

That memory twisted in his chest and spurred
him onwards faster and faster until his focus
was solely survival—his body's needs reduced
to breath, balance and determination. He added
another circuit to an already punishing regimen
before returning to the cabin, telling himself it
was for his own good and not because she was
there, waiting for him.

He took the steps, ignoring the twitches in
his thigh muscles, and stripped off all layers,
refusing to let his awareness go beyond the
boot room. His skin was already on fire, the

sweat pouring from his body from the exertion despite the minus temperature, cooling and raising the hairs on his arms. But in his mind's eye he saw Freya in the boot room yesterday, peeling off her clothes and, just like that, he was rock-hard and furious.

He threw on fresh clothes just to get to the bathroom and, taking a deep breath, pulled open the door to the cabin, scanning the space for signs of Freya. A coffee mug was missing and the dishes he'd washed up last night had been put away. She was awake but back in the room then. He frowned. When he finished with the shower they'd have to sit and talk. But first he needed hot water to soothe the muscles he felt already tensing up from the punishing morning run. Imagining the blessed relief of the powerful shower, he cut the distance to the bathroom in long strides.

He noticed that the shower had been used and a vague warning sounded in the back of his mind but, desperate to feel the heat of the pounding water on his skin, he ignored it. Turning on the shower, he stripped, stepped in and…leapt back from the frigid icy shards of water. Grabbing the rail to stop himself from slipping, his heart rate sky-rocketed and it had *nothing* to do with desire.

'Freya!' he howled before turning the air

blue with more expletives than he'd uttered in the last two years.

She had used up all the hot water. Hot water that, without the solar panels in play to heat the large tank, was reliant on the much smaller wood burner. A supply really only enough for one shower a day. He cursed again. He heard bare feet skittering across the floor outside the bathroom and hoped she'd have enough sense to keep herself out of his line of sight until he'd calmed down—which would probably be just in time for Gunnar to return to pick her up.

Gritting his teeth, he rubbed himself viciously with the towel before getting dressed. He had what he needed in the boot room, and he had what he wanted in the garage. Warm clothes and a damn good distraction.

He prayed to whatever gods of old were listening to give him patience as he stalked towards the outbuilding, not realising that it had been the first time he'd not thought of Enzo or the mission in months.

Freya had returned to the room after the most amazing shower she'd ever had. The power and heat of the spray blasted away the fog from the night before and she'd emerged pink-skinned, refreshed and determined.

Until she'd sorted through the clothes she'd

worn last night, finding her underwear scrunched into the pocket of the joggers, and clenched her teeth together. Having not hung it out as Kjell had ordered her to do, they still held the damp sweat from yesterday's exertion running back and forth between the cabin and helicopter in the snow. She'd thought he'd been punishing her, which was why she'd ignored him, but now she was very much regretting it. Contemplating confronting him without underwear—again—made her feel vulnerable but she would...

Kjell's yell shook the walls of the cabin.

Her head snapped round and she ran into the living area and stared at the bathroom door, her eyes growing rounder with each expletive. Only when she caught the Swedish word for cold did she realise what had happened and ran back to the room and just about resisted the urge to hide under the bed. She heard the bathroom door slam back into its frame and the stamp of heavy feet stalking towards the boot room.

'Freya—' his voice all growl '—keep the wood burner fuelled or there really will be trouble.'

The cabin door slammed, flinging another open in her mind.

Trouble, Freya. I'm nothing but trouble.

She walked out into the living area, des-

perately throwing up mental blocks against
the memory pushing at her mind. Her heart
trembled.

I don't want to remember. I don't.

She squeezed her eyes shut and clenched her
fists as if the physicality of it would hold her
in the present. But instead of the frigid dry
cold, she inhaled the damp scent of wet leaves,
pumpkin spice and autumn.

She pulled at the neck of the T-shirt, feeling
the warmth of the knitted scarf she'd thrown
about her neck before leaving her dorm room
to find him. To find Kjell.

*Her heart pounded in her chest as she ran
down the path she'd seen him on just seconds
earlier. She swept around the corner and came
to an abrupt stop at the sight of his back. The
tension cording his neck and shoulders told
her that he knew she was there.*

*'Kjell, please stop,' she begged, her breath
frosting the night air and catching the light
from the lamppost.*

*He did as she asked but refused to turn
around.*

'Kjell, that kiss—'

*'I shouldn't have done that.' He threw the
words over his shoulder, reluctant even then
to look at her.*

Her heart curled in on itself. 'Why not? Did you not—?' She broke off, hating the need in her voice. 'Did you not like it?'

'Freya...'

He turned and she could finally see the conflict in his gaze. Seeing the struggle in his eyes gave her courage.

'Kjell, I've done everything right. I've been the perfect Princess. I've done everything that was ever asked of me. I've never been in a tabloid, never been a headline. I've never put a foot out of line and I've never ever asked for something I've wanted for myself. Until now. Until you.'

'Trouble. Freya. I'm nothing but trouble.'

'I don't care, Kjell,' she cried.

'But I do, Freya! I care so damn much. I care that I can't be with you. I care that I can't like that kiss, or look at you the way I want to. I care that I can't touch you, or hold you, or do the things you beg me to do every time you look at me. So yes, Freya, I do care. You're a princess and even I know that you can't be with me. Your parents would never allow it.'

His eyes shone in the dark, the conviction, the hurt, the need.

'I know it's selfish to want this,' she said, closing the distance between them, 'to want you. And yes, I know it can't last,' she said,

feeling the sob in her chest like a physical ache. 'I know that this is all I'll ever have of you. But I'm asking you to give me this, knowing that it's selfish, that it's unbearably cruel to both of us, but knowing that I'd rather live the rest of my life with the memory of you than the regret of never having loved you.'

She *had* been selfish. It had been her. Her need that had driven it, driven them together. For two blissful months before it all came crashing down, she'd hoarded him like the most precious crown jewel. But she realised now that Kjell would never have laid a finger on her if she hadn't pushed at every turn. She'd been the one who had brought them together and he'd been the one who had paid the price.

An exile that had kept him from his family, his home, his country.

She rubbed at the chill that wrapped around her, arms rippling with goosebumps, her unseeing gaze slowly focusing on the snow falling beyond the window. He must have felt so alone. She frowned, the cold around her a little stronger now.

She looked at the wood burner and realised that it was running low. But scanning the room—she couldn't see any wood to fuel it. There was a box of kindling, but no logs.

Frowning, she looked again, shaking her head and hating that she was missing something painfully obvious. It made her feel…inept, not being able to do something as simple as adding wood to a fire to keep herself—and this room—warm.

After another five minutes she was beginning to get angry with herself for not finding the secret stash of wood and frustrated that she'd have to go and ask him. But she'd rather that than risk the fire going out.

She hurried to the boot room and found her boots. There were plenty of coats and jumpers, scarves and hats, but she looked at her clothes up on the drying rack near the ceiling and remembered. Stifling her embarrassment, she quickly washed her underwear in the sink and hung them up to dry.

Zipped up, tied up, wrapped up five minutes later, she pulled open the door and nearly shut it again. The blast of sub-zero air slapped her hard and fast and she had to lean into the wind just to stay upright.

Where was Kjell and what was he doing out here?

With one hand, she shaded her eyes from the furious frigid little flakes peppering her with icy accuracy, not even able to see the other cabin in the distance. Even knowing it was the height of madness, she was about to step out into the maelstrom when she noticed—with great relief—a pile of wood just on the inside of the porch. Pulling armfuls of the wood inside the boot room, she left a pile by the connecting door and took the rest straight into the cabin and nearly dropped them when she saw the fire had gone out.

'No, no, no!'

She fell to her knees by the burner and went to pull the door handle, yanking it back when her palm burned. Finding a set of gloves, she thrust them on, ignoring the burn, and yanked open the door, terrified by the hiss of smoke and barely glowing embers. In a panic, she grabbed a fistful of the kindling, threw it onto the bottom of the stove and thrust one of the big logs on top. Seeing some tiny little pellet things that must be firelighters, she grabbed two, then two more—just in case. There was a box of long-stemmed matches and as she struck one her fingers shook.

'Please let this work…*please*,' she prayed.

She placed the match beneath the first firelighter and then the second, before she threw the match into the belly of the wood burner. But her sigh of relief choked in the moment that the wood started to hiss and flare. Tiny little sparks like furious fireflies exploded into being and, panicking, she hastily shut the door to the burner. The spitting white specks zoomed for a little longer but then went out. Smoke began to fill the chamber behind the glass door. Freya didn't know what to do.

Gingerly she opened the door and thick dark smoke billowed into the room. Terrified, she shoved another load of firelighters into the burner and, waving the smoke out of her eyes, tried to light the fire. But the smoke wouldn't stop coming and the wood was making a terrible hissing noise.

A thick black fog was seeping into the cabin and Freya began to choke. Her heart in her mouth, she scrabbled back towards the door to the boot room. She ran for her boots, not even bothering to tie them up, shoved her arms into the nearest coat and ran out into the snow.

'Kjell!' she cried, not even sure what direction he was. If he was even nearby. She screamed his name again and suddenly firm hands grabbed her by the arm.

'Are you hurt?' he demanded, pink slashes on his skin, no hat on his head and his jacket as open as hers.

She shook her head. 'I'm so sorry!'

'Are you hurt?' he asked again, shaking her ever so slightly to cut through her fear.

'No. I'm okay. The wood burner,' she cried,

pointing to the cabin, where black smoke was coming out through the door she'd left open.

In three heartbeats he went from relief to fury to exasperated action. He realised exactly what had happened as he launched into the cabin, hating—absolutely hating—leaving the doors open, knowing how much invaluable heat was escaping.

Pulling his jumper up, he covered his nose. There was *so much* smoke.

She'd let the fire go out—that much was clear. He wanted to curse her, but really he was cursing himself. What would a princess know about keeping a wood-burning stove lit? He hadn't even shown her where the wood was kept. He eyed the storage box beneath his grandmother's knitted throw, which contained enough dry wood for two days, and just stopped himself from kicking the wet wood she'd brought in from outside. Fire out, damp wood? Just enough for a backdraught to knock out her attempts to relight the thing.

By the time he'd restarted the fire and ensured the dry wood was catching, he turned, expecting to find her beside him, but she wasn't. He exhaled a sigh of pure frustration. She was still outside.

Stubborn little princess.

They were going to have to clear the air—figuratively as much as literally—or things could get dangerous.

As commander of over six hundred soldiers, he knew how important communication was. And how deadly it could be when it was unclear. His stomach twisted and a cold sweat broke out on his neck. A sense of creeping panic rose as imaginary flashbangs exploded and screams sounded in his ears, but he willed it all away. Freya was the most clear and present danger at the moment. The ghosts could wait.

Gritting his teeth, he gathered himself for a confrontation that had been eight years in the making. He held back just for a second, watching her through the swirls and flurries of snow. Damn stubborn woman.

He could tell she was freezing from here. Making a quick assessment, he figured she'd need to be inside at least within the next five minutes or she'd be at risk of getting dangerously cold. Thankfully she'd grabbed his military jacket, thermal-lined for sharpshooting.

She was so beautiful, he thought as the snow raged and his conscience screamed at him to get her inside.

'Freya!' he yelled, beckoning her inside with a jerk of his hand.

She shook her head.

What was she playing at?

'Inside, Freya.'

'No!' she shouted.

This was not the time for her to be messing around. Her body was shaking and her lips beginning to bleed into blue and still her eyes spat fire.

'Why not?'

'Because you're mad at me.'

'Yes.' He didn't deny it. He was mad as hell. But it had very little to do with her failed attempts to smoke out his cabin and everything to do with what he wanted to do to her when he got her back in the cabin. None of which involved clothes and every one of them involved using up all this pent-up frustration between the two of them until it burned out completely.

'I can't… I just…'

'Freya, you're freezing. Just come inside,' he said, taking a step towards her.

'I'm n-n-not. I'm f-fine.'

'Freya, don't be difficult,' he said, knowing the statement would rile her.

'Kjell Bergqvist, do not sp-sp-speak to me like I… I'm a child!'

'Then,' he said, reaching her in easy strides, 'stop *behaving* like one.'

She glared up at him—haunting pale amber eyes flashing like Goldschläger. He could almost feel the alcohol burn his throat. It was enough. He bent his knees, wrapped his arms around her waist and hauled her easily over his shoulder. Spinning in the snow, he marched back to the boot room and kicked the door closed behind him.

'Are you going to behave?' he asked, trying so very hard to keep the laughter out of his voice.

'How *dare* you?' came her muffled response as her little fists pummelled ineffectually against his back.

'I'm not letting you down until you agree to stop sulking.'

She froze. 'I am not sulking,' she hissed.

He was a Lieutenant Colonel and he'd dealt with more recalcitrant new recruits than could be imagined. Waiting out one little princess who'd always had the patience of a gnat was easy. Not that he wouldn't keep her on his shoulder until the morning if he had to.

'I'm sorry.'

The whispered words caught at his heart, the sadness in them as unexpected as his instant re-action to them. He frowned and bent his knees so that he could let her down, the delicious fric-tion of her body against his lost momentarily in his concern for her.

'It's just smoke, Freya.'

'Not just about that,' she replied, her eyes

locked onto the corner of the boot room, plucking at his heartstrings as if it were hers to play.

And finally he did what he'd been wanting to do since she'd turned up at his cabin. He took her chin with his thumb and forefinger and gently pulled her round to face him. He wanted to see her eyes as much as he wanted her to see his.

'Your exile, Kjell—'

'I deserved nothing less,' he replied honestly. It had hurt him—devastated him—not to be able to see his parents. To know that he'd lost his father's respect. That day had been matched only by losing Freya. Ever since that day he'd done what he'd needed to. He could do his job, and do it well. He could laugh with his military brotherhood and he could live in whatever country he was sent to next. But being cut from the very things that made him feel connected to his past, to his family, his people… Freya— it was a phantom pain that he'd only realised when he'd returned. The familiarity that always rolled over him like a tsunami for those hours had made him realise just how *un*familiar the rest of his life was. Just how much had been taken from him.

But he'd also known that he deserved punishment for what he'd done. He'd broken a moral code in lying to her about his true identity but, worse, by giving in to the temptation of her he'd put her safety at risk. And that was untenable.

'No one deserves that, Kjell. Certainly not for this long. We were kids, we didn't know better.'

Everything in him wanted to roar in denial. He might have been young, but he'd known exactly what he was doing. Yes, he knew that lying was wrong, but Christ, he'd… his mind snapped, his teeth biting together, cutting off the train of thought before he could finish it.

His free hand clenched and he watched her eyes flick down to it and back up to him. Forcing himself under control, he offered the apology she'd not wanted to hear all those years ago.

'I'm sorry too,' he said, unable to stop his hand rising or his thumb sweeping gently across her jawline. 'I should have told you.'

'Why didn't you?'

'Because I wanted you more than I could stand,' he said, before letting her go and walking away.

CHAPTER FIVE

FREYA STOOD IN the boot room for long, long minutes after he'd left. Blinking slowly while replaying his words on a loop.

I wanted you more than I could stand.

Her pulse thundered in her chest as her mind assaulted her heart with images from their time together. Kisses, touches, laughter, love… The look in his eyes he would get sometimes when she caught him unawares. A kind of regretful longing. She'd not wondered at the time what had been on his mind, because she'd felt the same thing. Neither had been willing to admit that what they shared had an expiry date. Because even if he had told her the truth and even if they had spoken about it, the fact that she was a princess meant theirs was a future that could never have been.

In her hurt and anger, it had been easier for her to blame Kjell for the heartache than face the truth: that her status and her family would never have allowed him to become her consort. The thought of her father changing the legislation for her was as laughable as it was inconceivable.

And it was still in place, the decree that the consort for the first two legitimate heirs to the throne must have a title. It had been intended to protect the sanctity of the royal bloodline during a period when such things had to be unquestionable. None of her Svardian ancestors had needed or wanted to challenge the Royal Marriage Act since.

But if Freya was stepping down, then she would no longer be bound by that law.

Her heart raced as quickly as her mind.

I wanted you more than I could stand.

Blindly stripping off her coat and boots, she walked into the cabin, her insides trembling, unsure of what to expect.

Kjell was kneeling by the wood burner, feeding a log into the fire. He beckoned her over when he saw her, his gaze blank of the devastating emotional kick that he'd last looked at her with. She went to him, remembering this part of Kjell. His ability to shut down, switch tack, compartmentalise. It was probably what made him such a good soldier. She would get nothing further from him. Not now, anyway.

'So,' he said, his tone authoritative, 'if that happens again, you need to know how to start a fire.'

An hour later, and Freya was still watching the flames of the fire she'd help to build. Kjell was in the kitchen and the smells were making her stomach growl. She'd not eaten since the hastily grabbed bowl of cereal she'd had that morning, and she'd missed a meal last night. She could get a little like that. Henna always had snacks and protein bars in her bag, sneaking them to her in between appointments. Usually, every single minute of her day was planned out with precision, but here there was nothing to distract her thoughts from veering between the past and an unknown future.

But this was her second day here and she'd not thought once about the 'next' meeting, or checking the daily schedule to ensure she knew everyone's names, faces and enough about their lives to make the connections that were so important to her and to the success of her charities.

She inhaled, low and slow. The kind of peace that was found here... She understood why Kjell had chosen this as his home. But it was a sad sort of peace as she recognised that while she might have this calm in her future, it hurt to know that she would be saying goodbye to all the good she could do as a royal.

And, rather than dwell on it, she allowed herself to be hypnotised into an aching sort of restfulness by the falling snow. The wind was beginning to slow—the eddies and currents in the flakes less frantic, more graceful and she couldn't help but wonder what the windows revealed in the summer. Where, instead of shades of grey, the landscape would be awash with greens and browns, blues and yellows. To be able to sit here and watch the seasons change…

She heard a pan drop onto the stovetop and another Swedish curse. Peering around to the kitchen area, she saw Kjell shake his hand, angrily staring down at the offending cooking equipment.

'Can I help?' she asked as he rolled his shoulders back, the muscles rippling beneath the fine thermal jumper that pressed as close to his skin as she wanted to.

'Could you set the table?'

It was such a domestic moment it struck right to her heart. For a second she was frozen in place, remembering how they'd once laughed in her dorm room at university the first time Freya had ever set a table. He'd always had her doing things that were unfamiliar to her, from the smallest to the greatest. He'd always encouraged her. Another clatter came from the kitchen, thrusting her into action. As she went to the shelves that held stacked plates, glasses, mugs and cutlery, she couldn't help but ask, 'You still swear in Swedish?'

When she looked up she caught his gaze and something passed across his eyes.

'My father is Swedish,' he said, turning back to the large pan on the stovetop.

Then she remembered. 'Oh, I thought that was…' She trailed off, wanting to bite out her own tongue.

'Not a lie, Princess,' he said, his tone brutally bland.

She hated the twist of shame that unfurled at her implied accusation. She wanted it gone. This tension, this awkwardness. She wanted the ease that they'd shared all those years ago.

'My father is Swedish but moved to Svardia to be with my mother when they married,' he said, as if presenting the information as a peace offering.

'He gave up everything to be with her?' she asked, surprised. 'Why?'

'He loved her. And her job is…important.'

'What does she do?' Freya asked, beginning to ease into the back and forth of the interaction.

There was a pause and when she looked up his back was to her, his hands pressed against

the sideboard. 'She's the Principal Private Secretary of the Royal Household.'

Freya nearly dropped the plate she was holding. 'Anita Bergqvist? Your mother is—?'

'Yes.'

'Kjell!'

'What?'

'I see your mother almost on a daily basis!'
she cried, hating the feeling of pins and nee-
dles creeping across her skin, humiliation and
guilt vying to win out.

'And?'

'And doesn't she blame me for separating
her from her son?'

'I'd imagine she blames her son for making
a monumental mistake and getting himself exiled,' he ground out, stalking towards the table
with two bowls in his hand. 'The bread is on
the side, there's butter in the cool box under
the sink by the window.'

A monumental mistake.

If he only knew. Thinking of her diagnosis,
thinking of the future she would now have,
he'd had a lucky escape and just didn't know
it. He'd always been interested in her siblings,
not because of their titles but because of their
relationship. The bond, as loving and frustrated and downright painful as it was sometimes. She'd told him how much her brother's

retreat had hurt her, confessed that she had spoiled their sister sometimes but hadn't been able to help it. Kjell had relished every part of that because he'd relished *family*. By the time she returned to the table she thought she'd gathered herself, but the assessing gaze he sent her way made her think again. He'd always been able to do that. See the truth of her.

After placing the bread and butter on the table, she scooped up some papers and felt Kjell flinch as she placed them at the far end. Glancing down at the top of the pile, she saw an unfilled After Action Report with a due date of a week ago and felt her pulse leap.

Retreating behind a mask of innocence, she sat down and helped herself to dinner, while her mind tripped and turned over the report and Kjell's reaction. It *had* to be connected to the medal. But AARs were vital military assessments, to let one slide past the due date was... *wrong*. It just didn't fit with the by-the-book excellence that would have been required for Kjell to reach Lieutenant Colonel in such a short time.

To cover her thoughts, she returned to Anita. 'Your mother is wonderful,' she said, her tone infused with genuine warmth.

Kjell's gaze hunted her features for any sign of a reaction to the AAR. The realisation that she might connect it to the medal had overridden the wave of anger and shame he'd felt when he caught sight of it; the report was a rope around his neck tying him to things he needed to be free of. But Freya had shown no sign of recognising the documents or their importance and when she'd returned the conversation to his mother the honesty in her tone was clear.

'She is,' he said truthfully. Anita Bergqvist was the best of them all. He knew it and his father knew it. She loved everyone unconditionally and there was not a malicious or mean bone in her body. How his taciturn father had ended up with a wife like that Kjell would never know. His mother was—as Freya had said—wonderful. She was also incredibly good at her job and even though Brynjar had been a military man when they'd met he'd understood in his own way that her role was hierarchically above his and his complete and utter respect for chain of command made the choice to leave his career and country behind for Svardia an easy one. That and the fact that his father loved his mother completely. Kjell just wasn't sure Brynjar felt the same way about his son.

'Please don't tell me your father works in the palace too.'

He shook his head, swallowing a mouthful

of the stew before replying, 'Mechanical engineer for an aerospace company.'

'How did Anita meet an aerospace engineer?' Her tone utterly mystified.

'They met before, when my father was still in Sweden.'

'What did he do?' she asked as she buttered a thick slice of bread.

'He was an Överste in the Swedish Army.'

Her knife paused mid-swipe, and he felt her eyes on him. Assessing. Probing. Looking for more. Looking deeper.

'Following in his footsteps?'

Following the only thing his father had ever given him to cling onto. While his mother was all emotion, her love given freely with a kiss, a hug, an unconscious but ever-present touch, his father was the complete opposite. Monosyllabic and contained to the point where every gesture was small, efficient and practical, he rarely displayed affection or emotion and often retreated to his workshop to tinker with broken bits of machinery at even the mere hint of it.

When he'd told his father that he wanted to join the army it had been the first time he'd seen something like pride in his eyes. His father had placed a hand on his shoulder and Kjell had felt as if his heart might burst. But the day he'd told his father what had happened with

Freya, Kjell believed he'd felt that thin fragile thread between them break and it had hurt him more than Kjell could ever have imagined.

'Something like that,' he said, finally answering Freya's question, wanting to shift and twist away from the memories her questions conjured. 'How was Marit? After the accident?' He knew that she was okay, he'd not been living under a rock for the last eight years. But he knew how trauma could change a person.

'Worse, if you can believe it.'

Kjell couldn't help but smile. Freya had always been worried about her younger sister's tearaway tendencies.

'There we all were, terrified that she might not actually survive, and the first thing she said when she opened her eyes? *Can I go again?*'

Kjell saw past the mock frustration in her tone, knowing the depths of her love for her sister. With essentially what had amounted to absentee parents, Freya had easily and willingly slipped into that nurturing role, given the age gap between the two sisters. It had been a precariously balanced relationship, but one utterly filled with love.

'She never seemed the type to buckle down to royal duties,' he said, instantly stilling the moment he saw her tense—as if what he'd just said had hurt her in some way.

It was as if they were playing a game. On the surface were innocent questions, two old friends just catching up. Beneath that, though, was a darker, more dangerous current: one that tested and pushed at old wounds and new hurts.

'No,' she replied. 'But what about you? You've been with the UN? All this time?'

The swift turn in direction Freya executed proved his point. Mentally he applauded, while almost feeling sorry for her. Because he wasn't going to leave this table without discovering what it was she was hiding, and what it had to do with that damn medal.

Somewhere deep down a part of his soul cried foul, cursed him for using her vulnerability to avoid Enzo. To avoid the AAR. To avoid why he'd come out to Dalarna four months ago and not returned to active duty like the good soldier he was. But he'd spent a long time stifling that voice and Kjell only felt it as a gentle nudge on his conscience now. One that was easily ignored.

'Yes,' he answered her question, while working out how to turn the conversation around.

'Where were you stationed?'

'All over.' He shrugged, his mind on—

'Kjell.'

He pulled up mentally. She'd always done that. No one else ever knew when he split his focus between two different things, but she had. Every time.

'The UN has peacekeeping missions across the world,' he answered, deciding to play along for the moment. 'I've been to the Philippines for disaster relief, ceasefire observations in India and Pakistan, Kosovo for human rights, I spent a secondment with UNTSO in the Middle East.'

'Truce Supervision?'

He nodded, not surprised that she knew the different units and their roles. She might have cut him from her life and never looked back, but he'd not done the same. Some might have called it self-flagellation. Enzo had called it stalking. His body tensed, braced against a sudden wave of shocking grief.

'Kjell—'

'It's nothing, he said, interrupting her before she could ask if he was okay. She saw too much. She always had done.

He got up from the table, reaching for her bowl before he'd even asked the question. 'You done?'

Freya wasn't stupid. She knew that something terrible had happened and that it was wrapped up in the AAR and the medal. She could have throttled Aleksander: sending her here, knowing that she would do whatever it took to make Kjell accept the medal because she had no other choice was beyond cruel.

The ferocity of the silence Kjell pulled about him was, ironically, the most violent she'd ever seen him. The fight in him at that moment was real and vicious. And while knowing what had happened might make it easier for her to get him to take the medal, it was no longer self-interest that drove her. She couldn't see him hurt and not want to help. Her heart twisted to see him in such pain.

'Why won't you accept the medal?' The words were out of her mouth before she could stop them, but she would not call them back.

He turned from the sink and leaned back against it. 'Why is it so important to you?'

She stilled, trying not to betray herself. 'It's not.'

'Oh, Freya,' he said, all mock disappointment as he dried his hands on a towel. 'And there I was thinking that there were no more lies between us.' All that was missing was a tut-tut.

'I don't know what you mean,' she evaded, standing up from the bench, suddenly needing to get away from eyes that saw her too clearly, from a tone that needled her too much and a game she suddenly wasn't sure she wanted to play.

'You know *exactly* what I mean,' he said, stalking towards her, drawing close enough to trap her between the bench and the table, using his powerful shoulders to crowd her. He'd gone on the attack in the space of a heartbeat and she'd not been prepared. 'That little hint of desperation you get in your tone when you ask about the medal? The shadows shimmering behind your eyes…?'

She felt his gaze flick to the fluttering pulse beneath her jawline, its touch a physical thing. She knew the arrogant male smirk that pulled at his lips was a mask, even as her core muscles tightened. And lower. A pulse flared to life between her legs and she pressed her thighs together, trying to make it stop.

Not once had he moved his gaze from hers, but she knew he'd caught the movement, saw it in the flare of his irises, the heat that flushed his cheeks, matched only by that of her own. Flames licked up her spine and he'd not even touched her. Her breath caught and she was as unable to look away as she was to move. It was a sensual standoff, neither willing to back down or push them over the edge.

Skin humming and pulse throbbing, she hated that he'd done this to her. He was using her own body against her, to distract her from things he didn't want to answer, and somehow *she* was the one who couldn't escape.

Eight years ago, she had pursued him. Oh, she was under no illusions, it had been clumsy and even slightly awkward, but there had been a playfulness about it, a gentle innocence. Kjell's restraint then had required her to claim him for herself. But this? This power, this driving force Kjell had about him now...

Arousal built and built and built, flames pressing against the inside of her skin, wanting out, wanting Kjell. A fist was slowly tightening in her chest, squeezing her heart, her pulse flickering in its grasp. She couldn't not stare at his lips—the smirk having dropped ever so slightly from them, as if he too was caught in the vortex of their mutual desire. She bit her lip, hoping the sharp sting would cut through the sensual haze clouding her mind.

His gaze snapped to where her teeth pressed against the soft flesh and her breath shuddered in her chest. Fisting her hands, crescent imprints marred her palms as she fought not to reach for his shoulders, to mould them beneath her fingertips, to mark them with her nails...

She was shocked by the force of her want. Eight years had built fantasies and cravings she had never had the courage to consider all those years ago. Desires she was sure he could read in her eyes. Needs she felt pouring from her very soul.

They were barely an inch apart, his lips close enough to hers that if she moved even an inch… She closed her eyes in an act of surrender, of desperation, because she couldn't take it any more. The sensual tension pulling at her skin, her heart, her soul was too much to bear. He could have it. He could have it all.

But when the unspoken promise of his kiss never came, she only just managed to hold back the sob that racked her heart as much as her lungs. Shame, rejection, hurt, embarrassment swirled in a stomach already roiling from want. When she lifted her eyes to his, his cheeks were slashed with fury not need, his eyes spitting white sparks of indignation.

Kjell was trembling with rage. Seconds ago he'd felt a desire so intense, so powerful he'd never *ever* felt its like. But then she'd closed her eyes in submission and it had sliced through his arousal like the sharpest blade. She had sacrificed her agency in the one moment it would have meant the most, in the one moment they could have been *equals*.

He felt fury bleed into his gaze and prised his jaw loose enough to speak. 'I would never force a woman against her will.' His words were hoarse, as if he'd howled like the wolves that stalked the nearby woods.

'But I—'

He'd already seen the truth of it when she'd opened her eyes, and still she tried to evade him.

'What was that?' he demanded. 'Surrender?'

She turned away, shielding her eyes from his penetrating gaze, guilt written in red slashes on her cheeks. He shook his head in disgust. The tension and secrets between them were like an oil slick that turned his stomach.

Nothing felt solid any more. Ever since Enzo's death four months ago. As if he were still suffering from concussion, a dizziness that caused a slight delay, and Freya was only making it worse. More than just a friend, Enzo had been Kjell's tether. In a life that had so few constants, their friendship had been a bond that surpassed that of blood. To have that so cruelly taken from him had left him reeling in a way that he'd only ever felt once before. The night Freya had said she never wanted to see him again.

There was only one thing in that moment that would ground him, that he could grasp that would be real. He pressed forward, backing her up against the table without even having to touch her. 'Why do you need me to take the medal?' he said, the quietness of his words betraying the brutal demand in them.

'Aleksander needs—'

'Why do *you* need it?'

Freya paled and he wondered if she really thought he was so stupid not to have figured out that she had a stake in this. In the back of his mind a warning sounded. A dutiful soldier wouldn't push, wouldn't question. But maybe he was finally done being the dutiful soldier after all it had cost him over the years.

Enzo, home.

Her.

He drank in the sight of arousal shimmering beneath the secrets in Freya's eyes like a man dying of thirst. Her fingers gripped the table behind her, holding on or holding back, he couldn't tell. Didn't want to any more. His body inhaled the scent of her, warm and sweet on the air compressed between them, just as her head rocked back, exposing the long length of her neck. Their breaths fast and furious with need and desire.

He'd never stopped wanting her. It had always been there, in the back of his mind like a second heartbeat, just a millisecond out of sync. A shadow beat, constant and living, deep within him.

That was why there had never been anyone else. Ever.

It had only been her.

Rage and fury burned at the edges of his desire, inflaming his want and feeding his need and he hovered on the brink. But even if he gave into a temptation that could drive him beyond madness, even if they indulged in every whim he'd seen flash across her amber gaze—she was still a princess and he was just a soldier. She had always been out of his reach. As a young man he'd not realised what that meant, but the events of the last eight years had taught him well. So he marshalled his body with a ruthlessness that bordered on brutal and returned his gaze to hers.

As if sensing the shift in his focus, she averted her gaze, evidently more comfortable with her attraction to him than the secret she kept from him. And, like the trained hunter he was, he followed the trail of her deception.

'Why do you need me to take the medal, Freya?'

'I'm renouncing my royal title. And Aleksander will only let me go if you accept the medal.'

CHAPTER SIX

THWACK.

Kjell spun, kicking out at the punchbag hanging from the ceiling of the outbuilding. Despite the sub-zero temperature and the howling wind pounding the insulated walls, sweat dripped from his body. Squaring off against the sand-filled heavy bag, he threw his fists in a punishing combination ending—again—with another rounded kick, before landing comfortably on his feet.

I'm renouncing my royal title.

'Why?' he'd demanded, truly shocked for the first time since she'd turned up on his doorstep. She loved being a royal. She always had. You didn't have to know her to see that every time she was caught by a photographer, interviewed or overseas on a diplomatic visit, public service made her *shine*. She did her duty with the kind of grace that was innate, natural and genuine. Everyone commented on it, internationally and at home, and of all the royals Svardia's people would choose her again and again.

'It's none of your business.'

Thwack.

Her tone had been as cold as the icicles forming on the solar panels on the roof—and just as deadly to his peace of mind.

'It is when it's conditional on me accepting a medal I don't want,' he'd growled. 'Don't bother asking me again until you're ready to tell me what's really going on.'

Thwack. Thwack.

She'd stood there and stared him down until he'd finally stepped back to let her leave or risk becoming the kind of monster he'd claimed not to be. She'd slipped past him and the last thing he'd heard from her was the door to the bedroom closing behind her.

His fists were a blur, his knuckles long since numb beneath the wrap he'd wound around his fingers, palm and wrist. Leaning in to add an elbow to the combination, he felt sweat flick from his skin as he stepped back and planted his non-load-bearing foot into the centre of the bag, sending it high into the air, before striking it again on the backswing.

Ignoring the unfamiliar tremble in his arms, he cycled through the routine, sweat shining his skin and his pulse tripping.

She's not stupid, he heard Enzo observe in his mind.

No, Kjell thought. She wasn't. The Italian soldier would have liked Freya. A lot. Or he would have liked who she'd been at university. The years in between had made her...sharper. Less soft. Less giving. But no less stubborn. Dropping to the floor into a plank, he counted down from sixty.

'You have no sense when it comes to that woman,' Enzo said through his laughter.

Kjell smiled back as his team took some R&R in Bosnia. Eight of them, five men, three women, all of similar rank, sat round the table, drinking beer from ice-cold bottles under the umbrellas of the cobbled street café. War stories of the romantic kind were being shared because the real kind didn't really bear thinking about. Every single man and woman there had been shot at, near exploding IEDs, and had seen enough human misery to make even the hardest heart weep. And every single person at that table was staring at him as if he'd grown a second head.

'Really? Princess Freya of Svardia?' Suzu Kuroki asked.

Kjell considered it a feat to surprise the cool, calm intelligence officer from Japan.

Jean-Michel, a jarhead from France, slapped the table and laughed. 'No way, mon ami, no way!'

This was what he liked most about the UN secondments. It didn't matter whether a team had been together three days or three months, there was an understanding, a bond—a family. What was shared on downtime stayed on downtime, and Kjell never begrudged Enzo pulling out Freya to taunt him. He only ever did it when a team needed to let off steam, or just to laugh.

Sometimes Kjell would rip into Enzo about the beautiful Italian wife he'd left behind to bring up their two adorable children, dark-haired and dark-eyed, just like their father. Because there were times when they had to laugh or they'd go mad.

'You'll go to your grave with blue balls, my friend,' Enzo teased.

Kjell had promised to kill him for that.

Only he'd not had to.

On another continent, six months later, someone else had got there first.

Snowflakes were hurled on the raging wind, as helpless as confetti, their jagged trajectory as chaotic as it was fleeting. Freya sat in a nest of throws on the sofa tracing flake after flake, heart bruised and mind numb.

I'm renouncing my royal title.

She'd told him. She'd said the words. And the world hadn't ended.

It should have been a relief—a release, the confession that set her free. But, instead, it was the moment she'd realised the horrifying truth of it all: that this wasn't even the hardest part.

Freya thought of the calm she'd consciously wrapped herself in throughout the invasive tests and check-ups, the different hormone medications to thicken the womb lining. She had borne the mood swings, sweats and the horrifying feeling that her body wasn't her own with a serenity that befitted the perfect princess. She had allowed them to test her as if she were a faulty machine.

And when she'd overheard the doctor giving his final diagnosis to her *brother*, not her, as if her womb was more important to the throne than her as a person, as a woman, as a little girl who had always dreamed of having her own family…she'd clenched her jaw and said nothing. Because she understood that a king needed to know anything that affected the lineage. Because she knew—had always known—that her duty was first and foremost to that throne. Just like the doctor, just like her brother. And all three had known that the best way for her to do her duty was to step down, even if Aleksander still fought her on it.

Throughout it all, she'd believed that the hardest point would be renouncing her title. The sacrifice she would make to ensure that Aleksander's rule wasn't questioned or tainted by the fallout. Yes, there would be questions, but between Henna and the palace's communications team they would come up with a reasonable out. An out that would have them focused on her, not the fertility of their King or their younger sister. An out that wouldn't jeopardise all the good that her siblings could do for Svardia. Freya would do *anything* to make that possible.

But last night, when she'd finally revealed her intention to Kjell, she'd truly realised that facing the press, stepping down, wouldn't be the hardest part. It was what would happen *after*. After the furore died down, after the practicalities had been dealt with. It would be in a year, maybe two, when there was nothing left to fight, when there was no one around and she had to finally face the fact that her body was broken and she'd never have what she'd always wanted to have.

The hurt in her heart made her selfishly want to reach out to Kjell for comfort. A comfort that, no matter the years of distance, the pains of the past, she still felt was possible between them. The familiarity of him, even in spite of the changes, of the man he had become, a hope in her soul. But the tension between them was a reality she couldn't ignore. And his demand one she couldn't deny.

Don't bother asking me again until you're ready to tell me what's really going on.

She knew him well enough to know that he was serious. He wouldn't settle for anything less than the truth now. She hated that she would have to tell him. And it was so much easier to hold onto that anger, the fury at the injustice of it all, after everything that she had sacrificed, all the good she had done, it raged in her heart.

A rage that demanded to be heard. It scratched along her skin and clawed at her chest. She wanted to howl at the moon, it was so unfair. It was so horribly unfair. A strange, determined fury fizzed in her veins, unpleasant but invigorating. It pushed away the numbness and made fissures in the serene mask she had made of her features. It broke and shattered the façade into a thousand pieces.

And now, staring at the fading shadows bleeding across the snow, she knew only that the seal on her anger had finally broken. And it was all coming out. The pain, the hurt, the shame, the anger, the fury.

Don't bother asking me again until you're ready to tell me what's really going on.

She flicked the tears away from her cheeks as she thrust herself into her own clothes, now dry in the boot room. Her shaking fingers were barely able to tie the laces of her boots, and she just remembered to grab a scarf as she launched from the cabin towards the outbuilding where she knew Kjell was.

Wind battered her, snow pelted her, but *she* was the wild one here. She felt the elements rise up within her to match the fury of the storm raging around her. Through the swirls and currents of the snow, she could make out the door to the outbuilding and was still too angry, too untethered to feel anything other than grim determination to confront the man behind the door.

Kjell spun round when the door flew open, his pulse still pounding in his ears from the brutal workout. Freya stormed into the outbuilding, slamming the door shut behind her, as angry as he'd ever seen her.

'You want to know why I need to step down?' she shouted at him. She looked incandescent and devastatingly gorgeous with it.

'Yes!' he yelled back, turning to face the fury coming towards him full-on. He welcomed it, the anger, the challenge—but if he'd thought it would cut through the desire he felt for her, he had been very wrong. Instead, it only inflamed his need. Too much had been kept locked away for too long. Something had to give.

She came to within kissing distance, their breaths clashing in an unsustainable rhythm. She looked at him, shaking her head as if he was wrong, as if she knew that he didn't really want to know.

It was the first inkling he had that something was very, very wrong. This was worse than the night of Marit's accident, but he honestly couldn't imagine what it could be. Freya was shaking with rage and he wanted it unleashed. He'd take every single blow, every strike she could give him if it meant release from whatever terrible hurt held her in its grasp.

'I can't have children.'

His mind flatlined. There was a high-pitched whine in his ears and no thoughts in his mind. It was the last thing he'd ever expected her to say.

A knife ripped through his heart for her. His eyes widened in shock, his mouth jammed shut in the next heartbeat, to prevent pointless words from refuting her statement. This woman—

Freya—she had been made to be a mother. Everything in her nurtured, cherished, encouraged. She… He clenched his teeth together. Words of comfort streamed through his mind and he knew that none of them would help her in that moment.

'Okay,' he said.

'Didn't you hear me?' she demanded.

He nodded, the act ripping through the tension cording his neck muscles and shoulders. 'Okay,' he said again. There were so many words pressing against his heart and lips, but he wouldn't let them out. Couldn't. It wasn't about him, words that would make *him* feel better by appeasing *her* hurt.

'I said I can't have children, Kjell. I can't produce the heirs to the throne. The family's future is uncertain until Aleksander has children. And Marit—'

'Stop it,' he ordered, hating the excuses and distractions she was covering her pain with. Her pretty mouth snapped shut and his heart broke a little more.

'Try again,' he growled, angry with her but most definitely angry with himself. He should never have pushed her. He didn't have that right. He should have known better.

'Try what, Kjell? You want me to parade my hurtabout for your amusement?'

'Freya, you know me. You know that's not what this is. You know *me*. So don't you dare give me the party line. Tell me where it hurts. Where it *really* hurts,' he said with a desperation in his eyes he knew she could see. He would never be able to take that pain away from her, but he would damn well die trying.

The confusion in her haunted amber eyes made him curse. Had no one asked her?

'Everywhere,' she whispered helplessly as tears brimmed in her eyes.

He couldn't protect her from this. It was a horrifying, stark realisation that gutted him to his core. He might have been a soldier for most of his life, but he never had and never would stop guarding her.

He reached up to cup her face, his thumb delicately sweeping to catch the tear that had tumbled over the edge. She leaned into his palm, her closing eyes sending more tears, too many for him to catch, down her cheeks.

He shut off the part of his mind that fixed, that planned, that created counter-moves and attacks. It wasn't time for thoughts of surrogacy, adoption, insisting that she didn't need to renounce her royal title or duties. If Kjell was right, then he'd imagine her brother would have tried that. No. This moment, right now, was about Freya.

He brought her to his chest, his hand gently tangling in her hair, his body absorbing shudder after shudder, but sending out heat to warm the chill of her skin, of her body—not from her clothes. It was a cold that went bone-deep. It was one he knew well. Shock. Mindless shock.

'Tell me,' he commanded, his voice barely a whisper. But he knew that she'd heard, that she'd understood.

'I fear that…that I'm not a woman any more.'

If he'd thought his heart had hurt before, it was decimated by the pain and devastation in that confession. A curse ripped through him and he drew her away from him gently, just so that he could see her eyes. Eyes that were full of evasion, shame and hurt. The torture he saw there would have broken even the strongest man and it had his soul raging.

Forcing his tone to gentle and his hold to soften, he pressed his forehead to hers. 'Yes, you are.' His words were low, soft and a promise he hoped she could feel the truth of.

'I don't know if I believe that any more.'

'What do you need to believe again?' he asked. 'What do you need?'

I don't know.

The unspoken answer ate at him, tearing him up. But as he searched her face for signs of what he could possibly give her, he saw the change in her eyes. Felt it like a primitive knowledge deep within him, an elemental reaction to her that had always been there.

As if for the first time, he realised how close they were. He could see the gold flecks in her amber eyes sparking and flashing, the blood began to rise through the paleness of her skin to slash her cheekbones in pink. Just the sight of it ignited his arousal and he tried to leash it, forcing it back nearly broke him but now wasn't the time. Freya needed him to be more than the horny youth he was reverting to. His hands released their hold on her and he stepped back to try to get himself back under control. She deserved better.

Her amber eyes turned molten and he fisted his hands to stop himself from reaching for her.

'Ask me again.' Her words fell between them—his heart balanced on a knife-edge. He wasn't a fool. He knew her want as well as he knew his own.

Don't do it. She deserved better. So much better than him.

'Kjell?'

He couldn't deny her. He had never been able to and he never would.

'What do you need?' His voice ragged with a desire unquenched in eight years.

'You.'

He clenched his teeth, knowing that it was madness but more than willing to lose himself to such a delicious insanity.

'Then take what you need,' he growled. 'Take me.'

The temptation in her eyes inflamed his need, but still she held back.

'If this is about pity—'

'Pity?' he echoed, taking her hand and pressing it against the length of his arousal, so eager for her touch it jumped beneath the heat of her palm. 'Does that feel like pity to you?'

Freya shook her head, shocked to silence by the feel of him in her hand. Wicked heat crept up her spine, licking and laving its way across her skin. A desperate need built and stretched, filling her so completely there was no thought of anything else.

Take what you need.

Could she? Could she lose herself in him?

No. She could never use him like that, just as he hadn't been able to consider anything but willing participation the night before. But neither of those things were happening now. She might not want to name it, not be ready to acknowledge the ties weaving between and around them, but it was definitely more than a distraction.

He had offered her solace. A solace that required trust. And she knew in that moment that she trusted Kjell more than anyone else in the world, no matter what had happened in the past.

Her fingers flexed around the deliciously familiar shape in her hand. Because, no matter what she'd told herself during the waking hours, no matter how much she thought she'd removed Kjell from her life, her night-time fantasies had always betrayed the truth. She had never forgotten him. *Any* of him.

She felt him tense against the wave of need that rippled through his body. His thigh muscles braced against an instinctive desire to move towards her.

'Freya.' Her name on his lips was a prayer, a curse, a warning she paid absolutely no heed to. Instead, it was one she welcomed. He had offered himself to her but, like him, she wasn't interested in anything less than willing participation.

She gripped him through the soft material of his workout joggers, the heat of him flooding into her skin even through the material, her thighs clenching at the thought of him entering her, sliding deep into her welcoming heat, a thought made even more sensually torturous by the knowledge of the pleasure she knew he could bring.

His hands fisted, knuckles white, and she knew she was pushing him towards a line in the sand. He was only doing this for her. But she didn't want to be the pyre on which he threw himself. They had both sacrificed enough. And the only way she knew to bring him into this was to push. And push and push. If they were going to break, then it would be the most exquisite way to shatter.

She raised up on her tiptoes and pressed an open-mouthed kiss against his firm lips. Her chest pressed against his, the stiff peaks of her nipples indulging in the delicious friction of her jumper and his T-shirt. Her tongue laved against the thick, full bottom lip and nipped gently at it until his mouth opened for her. But, instead of sweeping into his mouth, just as she sensed his capitulation, she drew back, her body, her soul hating her for it.

'Why are you teasing me?' he whispered, her heart nearly crippled by the vulnerability of his question.

She took a breath, hoping to hell that her next words were rally rather than retreat.

'Because I want *you*. Not the dutiful soldier.'

Just like that the heat in his eyes flamed out and she thought she'd lost him. Until he pulsed in her palm and she gasped. He gave her one more second to luxuriate in the feel of him, the strength of his need *for her,* and then batted her hand away, stalking forward and forcing her to step back. Again and again until she was pressed up against the work bench that ran along the edge of the room.

This predatory male was so different from the younger Kjell she had known, but absolutely no less dangerous to her senses. This. *This* was what she'd wanted. What she'd seen glimpses of in the last few days. This was what made her feel like a woman.

Her heart pounded in her throat as if it wanted to leave her body and meld with Kjell's. He pinned her with a lethal focus that was nothing short of an adrenaline injection straight to her heart. Her skin was on fire from the layers and layers of outdoor clothing that felt constricting to the point of painful.

Their breaths comingling in the narrow space between them, he reached up to the scarf and slowly slid it from around her neck. She gripped the bench behind her, holding herself up, holding herself *back*.

He cocked his head to one side as if daring her to stop him.

She didn't. She couldn't.

His gaze dropped to her lips and she bit

down instinctively, enthralled when she saw his swift inhalation. One final step brought his chest against hers, her breasts finding purchase against his body and delighting in the friction. Eyes still on her lips, his hands gripped the heavy-duty material of her borrowed jacket, as if torn between using it to pull her to him or pushing it from her body.

And then, finally, as if giving up the fight, his head bent to hers and he feasted on her lips. Her heart soared and her soul cried out for more as she opened to his possession, welcomed it, needed it. His lips demanded it all. This kiss was like nothing they'd ever shared before; it was a rending of the past, the present and the future all in one.

Pulling back from the kiss, he looked as shocked as she felt. Her breath shook in her lungs. 'I thought I was supposed to take what I needed,' she said, her voice trembling with desire, a shiver of want rippling down her spine and sheening her skin with need.

'You were taking too damn long—' his words short and sharp '—I'm just going to have to give you what you need.'

Her breath whooshed from her lungs as he scooped her up as if she weighed nothing, spun and walked them back over to the opposite side of the room.

'I should take you back to the cabin and strip you bare before the fire and the wildness of the woods,' he said, claiming her lips with more punishing kisses. 'But I can't wait that long.'

'Wait for what?' she asked hazily, her gaze heavy-lidded with desire.

'A taste of you,' he said, laying her carefully on the soft workout matting as if completely lost in his need to satiate a craving he'd had for years. He pushed the jacket from her shoulders and, instead of coming back to kiss her, he reached for the band of her leggings. She instinctively lifted up, allowing him to sweep them over her backside and down, just as she realised his intention.

Her heart thundered in her chest as he pulled her panties halfway down her thighs, a self-consciousness building in her until…

Until she saw the way Kjell looked at her.

Stark desire had slashed his cheeks red, his arctic blue eyes on fire. He might not have moved a muscle, sitting back on his haunches, his eyes raking over every inch of exposed flesh, but there was nothing still about him. The energy, the need—for her—raging beneath his skin was electric. She had done that to him. And he let her see it. He'd opened himself up to her to show her the effect she had on him.

A whimper rose in her that had nothing to do

with attraction and everything to do with a hurt beginning to heal. But the sound cut through whatever held Kjell back and, leaning back, he lifted her thighs apart, possessively positioning himself between them.

'Kjell,' she whispered.

'Changed your mind, Princess?' he taunted, wickedness in his gaze.

'Give me what I need,' she demanded hotly and the look in his eyes changed to something like pride.

'Yes, ma'am.'

CHAPTER SEVEN

FREYA'S LEGS TREMBLED so much on the walk back to the cabin, Kjell needed to scoop her up and carry her to the boot room. At least that was what he told himself, as if he didn't know that he couldn't keep his hands off her, even for that short walk.

She'd orgasmed on his tongue, around his fingers, and he'd never felt anything more exquisite in his life. The sweet taste of her hadn't been enough. *More*. He wanted more.

Insatiable, she'd said—the laughter in her voice true music to his ears.

He couldn't disagree. But he'd not lied when he'd told her that he wanted her naked in front of the fire in the cabin. He refused to make love to her there in the outbuilding on his exercise mat. Wasn't ruling it out later on, but that wasn't how he intended their first time in eight years to be. Because there was no fighting it any more.

The line had been obliterated and he had no intention of redrawing it.

But that didn't mean they didn't have to talk first.

He watched her unlace her boots, the flush of desire still bright on her cheeks, and when she looked up, grazing her gaze against his, the amber in her eyes glowed gold and he had to stop himself from reaching for her.

Roughly pulling at his outer layers, he watched her sweep into the cabin with a very feminine swish to her hips. It was only when he was alone that he allowed the sensual haze to dissipate enough to try to gather his thoughts.

In his mind he was back on the university campus green. Their studies had been interrupted by a frisbee that had scraped the top of Freya's head. The parent of the child had taken one look at her, eyes wide, offering profuse apologies.

It had taken Freya at least five minutes and a selfie to assure him that they weren't all going to end up in prison.

'That was kind of you,' he noted with a smile.
'Not at all. I'm earning good karma.'
'What for?' he asked on a laugh.
'For my children. They're going to terrorise

*the palace. I'll make sure of it,' she said with
such glee he felt it in his heart.*

*'Children?' His heart thudded in his chest—
painful, slow, heavy beats. Because they
wouldn't be his. Couldn't be.*

'Three.'

*She almost shone...until clouds formed in
her eyes.*

'And none of them will be a spare.'

Back in the boot room, back in the present,
Kjell clenched his jaw, his heart once again
aching for the children that Freya felt she'd
never now have. But he couldn't help but wonder if she was blinkered, as if those around
her so focused on bloodlines and lineage had
clouded what *could* be. And it was a conversation they needed to have before she went too
far to take it back.

He pushed into the cabin to find her staring
at the stunning view. She was framed by falling
snow, snow-covered trees—the natural wildness was stunning, but nothing compared to
her innate beauty. And while his pulse picked
up and desire flared anew, he forced it back.

'We need to talk.'

'I don't want to,' she said, her body instantly
stiff with a tension that had nothing to do with
desire or need.

He couldn't help but smile at the petulant tone he remembered well from eight years ago. He didn't want to cause her any more pain, but he knew her well enough to know that she'd probably not thought about her situation beyond the impact it would have on her family. He could have cursed them. Surely at least one of them had reassured her that she was more than just her worth to the throne.

'When did you find out?' he asked, coming to stand behind her, reaching out to snare her hips with his hands, delighting in the friction as she spun to face him.

She rose on her tiptoes, seeking his lips, but he leaned back from the reach of her kiss. Before, he'd been a willing distraction to take the edge off the raw pain in her heart. But now she needed something else, whether she wanted it or not. But that didn't mean he couldn't make it pleasurable. His hands held her in place and she scowled.

She turned her head away, purposely cutting him, but the smooth skin of her neck was exposed and he bent to press open-mouthed kisses, sucking gently, tempted to brand her as his but just managing to resist.

'I'll make a deal with you,' he offered. The stillness of her body told him he had her attention. 'For every answer you give me, I'll give you something in return.'

'Something?'

He smiled into the kiss he pressed to her collarbone. 'You'll have to answer a question to find out, Princess.' He waited, withholding his touch to see if she would take the bait. He saw her pulse flicker delicately at her jaw.

'Confirmation happened a month ago,' she said and in return he drew his palms up to either side of her chest and swept his thumbs over her nipples, teasing them into stiff peaks. She pressed into the pressure gently and gasped.

'But you've suspected since...'

She flicked her gaze to him and back over his shoulder as if punishing him. 'I first went to the doctor a year ago.'

'Should you have gone sooner?'

The aching thought that she'd neglected herself as she had done even back then during university was a low throb in his heart.

She stared at him, an eyebrow raised, reminding him that he owed her and, smiling, he freed a hand to reach for her chin, thumb and forefinger angling her face to perfection. He teased her lips with brushing kisses, his tongue testing the seam of her mouth until she opened for him. His pulse raised to new heights as soft wet heat welcomed his tongue, until she nipped at his lower lip startling his eyes open to see mischief shining back at him.

'No. I had… Do you really want to hear this?' she asked, the wound audible beneath the cover of exasperation.

'Yes.'

She sighed, the sadness in it hurting him deeply. 'I've always had irregular periods. They were frustrating, but manageable, especially as I was on contraception. Two years ago I decided to come off it but the irregularities increased, rather than settling down.'

Freya forced herself to keep going. There was nothing wrong with talking about a natural body function. If more people spoke about it freely, then maybe there wouldn't be such stigma. Such ignorance. Such awkwardness. Such *shame*.

'There was pain?'

'Yes.'

When he ran his hands over her body in payment for her answer it took some of the sting out of the conversation. As if he'd known that this was what she needed, known that this was the only way she could speak about it at all. His lips pressed down between her breasts, the heat of his breath warming her skin through the cotton of her long-sleeved top.

'Tests?'

'Yes. Invasive ones.'

His hand swept down to cup her backside, lifting her slightly in a way that pressed her against his erection, leaving her in no doubt of his desire for her, distracting her from thoughts of cold, sterile equipment and gloved hands.

She gasped as his hand swept between her legs, as if he were replacing bad memories with new ones, better ones.

'They revealed that the lining of my uterus was thin. It was the cause of the irregularities and—' she almost laughed at the cruel irony '—I was thankful that it was nothing more troubling. Until they told me that it would be impossible for an embryo to implant there. Impossible for me to carry a child to term. They tried increasing the hormones, but their effect on the lining was negligible.'

The press of his lips slowed and he pulled back to look at her. She read the next question in his eyes.

'They don't know why. There was no previous infection or scarring. It's most likely always been that way.'

She forced herself to meet his gaze as his fingers played with the hem of her top, lifting it up and over her head and casting it to the side. Stripping back the layers of her hurt just like her clothing should have made her feel weak, vulnerable, but instead the way he looked at her, the pure desire glowing in his eyes made her feel bold, feminine, *strong*.

'Why do you have to renounce your title?' he asked.

She was about to answer when his hands stroked and moulded her breasts with possessive sweeps of his palm and her mind sought to lose itself in his touch rather than answer his question.

'Freya...' he nudged her.

And he tightened his hold as she clenched her jaw against the sudden tide of anger returning to wash against her heart. 'They will crucify me.'

A frown slashed across his brow, his eyes blazing with fury. 'Who will?'

'The press. The people. They will never let me forget,' she said, her soul shaking with her deepest fear. 'Not only that, it will taint my family. They'll question the fertility of my brother, my sister... They'll study the family tree, looking for signs and symptoms of this biological failure that I will come to represent.' She knew how bad it would be. She had been the perfect princess and still she'd felt the shocking lash of their censure if a camera had caught her in an unflattering angle. Heaven forbid anything worse.

'Freya—'

'Have you ever read what has been written about Princess Masako? The Duchess of York? Queen Letizia? Princess Diana? The Princesses of Monaco? The Duchess of Sussex? Princess Madeleine? The press can and often will be cruel, critical, snide, malicious...until they produced a child. Do you know that on any internet search, on any biography, info page or description, the first thing that is listed after a princess's official title is the number and names of their children? Every. Single. Time. As a princess, I have *one* job. And it's not one I will ever be able to fulfil.'

'You say that they'll never let you forget, that it will become your identity. But can't you reclaim that identity? Make it your own on your terms? Control the—'

'Narrative? I don't want to have to!' she cried. 'It's hard enough as it is. And you want me to be the poster child for infertility? The guiding light, leading by example, taking all the flack for future generations of royals?'

'Not just royals... There are people out there without the support that you have.'

'You don't get to make me feel guilty about this,' she warned, her stomach churning.

'I'm not trying to, Freya, honestly. But there are so many options available to you, I just don't want you to make a decision that you can't take back. What is the urgency? Can you not wait a little longer until you've made peace with how you feel about it?'

'No. There isn't time. Not for Aleksander. Or Marit. Svardia needs stability. Right now. And although it will be hard stepping down, much better for it to be seen as my selfishness than anything that would undermine the royal family.'

He pierced her with a penetrating gaze. 'Or are you just clinging to that so you can burn it all down?'

She hated it that he was even just a little right, and—worse—that he could see that about her. It might be brutal but turning her back on it all was so much easier than trying to grasp at what was left.

'You want me to expose my damage to the public, but what about you?'

Kjell became preternaturally still.

'No? Nothing to say to that?' she demanded, hurt and anger making her cruel. 'About why you won't accept the medal? About what happened to require an After Action Report?'

He didn't turn away but his eyes on hers had become fierce. Their gazes flaying lies like layers of skin to reveal the deepest, darkest truths and hurts. Until they both chose to burn on a different fire, an easier one but no less passionate.

They came together in a punishing kiss. Brutal, crushing and utterly delicious. Teeth clashed with tongues, pulses pounded and palms pressed desperately against hot fevered skin. Freya revelled in the power of their desire—the incendiary heat between them burning away the hurt, the sadness, the ache deep within her that she feared might never be healed, no matter what her future. But all thoughts fled when she felt Kjell's fingers dip beneath the vest top and slide it up and over her head. The arctic blue gaze burned white-hot when he saw what he'd revealed of her, his eyes devouring her and seeming to glory in every inch of her body.

He leaned over her, pressing feverish lips to her skin and she couldn't help but arch into his caress, gasp as his tongue toyed with her nipple and whimper when he palmed her other breast. Heat, intense, damp and urgent, built between her legs, shocking and already sensitised after the intensity of her earlier orgasm.

His hand around her back dropped to grasp her backside, moulding her to him and the evidence of his own arousal.

'Perfect,' he whispered against her lips. 'You're absolutely perfect.'

His words turned in her heart and she wanted to be that. Perfect. For him. But before she could say so he gathered her up in his arms. Instinctively wrapping her legs around his hips, he lifted her, finally bringing them eye to eye, lip to lip, where the supremely arrogant male smirk made her smile.

'I wanted you like this,' he said. He must have seen the confusion in her eyes. 'From the first second I saw you, I wanted you naked, amongst the furs in front of the fire. I wanted it so badly.'

The confession felt precious, felt raw and honest—and she closed her mind to the part that warned that Kjell still hadn't trusted her with his hurt. But she needed this just as badly and she promised herself that it was enough. For now.

Kjell backed up to the sofa, holding her to him with one hand, drawing several of the furs onto the floor with the other, without breaking the kiss.

'Now you're just showing off,' she said against his lips, laughter in her voice and on the tongue that played with his when she'd finished taunting him and he thanked whatever deity was out there.

Her hurt, the fear that haunted her, had undone him. He couldn't stand to see her in so much pain. If he could have taken it from her, he would have. In a heartbeat. But he couldn't. So he'd do this instead. He'd distract her with pleasure and tease her with desire. And if a part of him called him a coward for hiding in that same pleasure, then he'd own it. There was a time and a place for his story, but now wasn't it.

'You wound me. That is hardly showing off. I could bench press you,' he said in between kisses.

She pulled back to stare at him.

'Really, I could absolutely—'

She scrambled down his body before he could show her and he held back the laugh bubbling in his chest. How they could go from tearing strips off each other to tearing off clothes in just a matter of minutes was incredible to him.

But not as incredible as the sight of Freya standing there before him, unashamed of the body that had caused her so much hurt. He couldn't look at her enough, his eyes running over every inch of her, committing her to memory.

The finest merino wool clung to her legs, displaying the powerful curves of her thighs, and he wanted to turn her around so that he could see how it sculpted her backside. He cursed. He was getting hard just looking at her. A blush rose to her cheeks as if she could see.

'Take it off,' he said, his tone guttural even to his own ears.

She looked for a moment as if she might argue, but then those incredible amber eyes melted to lava and instead she hooked her thumbs into the waistband and slowly, *too* slowly, peeled it down from her hips, her thighs and to her ankles before stepping out of it and throwing it aside.

He was about to speak when she beat him to it, with a wryly raised eyebrow, her thumbs catching on the thin lace of her panties and lowering barely an inch before pausing in this new game that had sprung between them. His heart pounded in his chest, on the knife-edge of a pleasure just within reach. He'd never stopped wanting her. Not once.

'Your turn,' she said, nodding to the top he'd worn for training. She'd barely finished her sentence before he practically tore it from his body. She was doing a terrible job of hiding her amusement, but when her eyes refocused on his chest the laughter died on her lips. Her gaze scoured him. He wondered what changes she'd see in his body after eight years apart. It hadn't taken him long in the army to fill out to a breadth that was as impressive as his height and without an ounce of pride he knew he was very different to the boy she must remember.

'You want me?' she asked, as if afraid that he might say no.

'I've never wanted anyone else.' The truth flying from his lips as if it had always belonged to her.

'Yes, but there were others,' she stated, trying so hard to hide the bite of jealousy that was easy for him to read. She was so sure.

'No.'

Her eyes flew to his in shock. 'What? Never?'

'It has only been you,' he growled.

It will only ever be you. The words cried out silently in his soul.

She took a step towards him, the finest tremor to her legs as if she was as affected by his confession as he'd been making it. He fisted his hands to stop himself from reaching for her. This had to be for her. She had to take what she needed and wanted.

She drew to a stop, barely an inch from his body, the heat from her skin washing against him like a tide, pulling him towards her against his will.

Her hand raised and swept a lock of hair from his forehead, her fingers shockingly cool against his face. Her hand trailed downwards, across his jaw, his neck and coming to a rest over his heart.

'Me too,' she said and, before he could process the hint of sadness there, she kissed him so passionately he couldn't hold back any more.

He swept her up into his embrace and knelt, placing her on the furs to satiate the incessant need that had thrown images of her just like this into his mind again and again and again. The fire blazed in the wood burner, casting flickering shadows over her deliciously warm skin. Outside, snowflakes were swirling and falling in a moving curtain, letting through the dusk, and welcoming the oncoming dark of night. But the strange haunting white glow reflecting from the snow made it feel as if they were in a magical land—one stolen from time, a precious second chance that seemed as impossible and fleeting as it was real.

Freya stared up at him from the furs, her earthy skin perfect against the deep russet and browns surrounding her. She reached for him and he couldn't deny her. He came over her in a kiss that stole his breath and his heart, only to find himself smiling barely a second later as she pushed impatiently at the waistband of his trousers. He was naked by his second breath and pure male pride burst to life when he saw the glare of desire flare in her whisky-coloured eyes at the sight of him.

Pulling him into yet another kiss, her body came to life beneath his, her legs parting to welcome him between them, her thighs shifting beneath his hips, and he couldn't help but run his hand between them to cup her wet heat. Her head drifted back, exposing her neck to his lips as he pressed open-mouthed kisses to her skin and pressed his thumb to the delicate flesh that sent Freya wild. He circled her clitoris before sweeping towards her entrance, gently teasing the heated dampness until she punished him with a bite to his bottom lip.

He smiled into her kiss as he gently drew himself down her body, settling between her thighs, where he could die a very happy man. Her hips twisted under his focus, drawing his gaze to where Freya watched him, pink-cheeked and breathless.

As his tongue swept out and she shuddered from the sensual kiss, he knew he'd never seen anyone or anything more beautiful in his life than Freya. He would have spent every day of it worshipping her, if he'd been able. But a relationship between them would never be allowed. He wasn't stupid, even this was a stolen moment. The truth was, a Svardian soldier could never marry his princess.

But she doesn't want to be a princess any more.

She did, though. She loved doing what she did and he knew it. And she would realise that eventually. But until then...

Her legs shifted again and he turned to take a gentle bite from her thigh, smiling at the peal of giggles that sounded like music to him. Then he couldn't help himself. He pressed kisses to the inside of her legs, easing into the space she created as she spread them for him. Slowly he drew himself up, kiss by kiss, until he could feel her beneath the entire length of his body. She moulded herself against him, dips filling hollows, curves claiming arches, the feel of her skin like silk.

She reached up to frame his face with her hands as he positioned himself at her entrance. The trust, the need and the sheer honesty he could see in the warm whisky-coloured eyes humbled him. And they rode out the moment together before he slowly entered her, the wet heat welcoming him in a delicious sensuous glide that had Freya gasping on an inhalation.

She surrounded him in a slick grip that held him tight and urged him on, urged him deeper. His mind filled with stars and his heart hurt at the beauty of what he was feeling. Of what he might never feel again. His arms, braced either side of her, began to shake as he held himself while she adjusted around him. The air between them filled with little sighs and pants as she relaxed around him, making him even harder within her. She bucked her hips gently beneath him and he wanted to curse, he wanted to pray. And when they started to move together he was simply mindless.

Freya was drowning in pleasure, gasping through it for air, for something more, something indefinable. As Kjell moved within her she became incoherent with need. That need a physical thing in her chest, growing, expanding, building and desperate for more, for *him*. It wanted out. It wanted release. And she could see that same need in Kjell's eyes as he stared down at her in wonder. She knew. She felt it. That incredulity that something—*anything*—could be this…incredible. Until that need became so all-consuming that it pushed her right to the edge.

'Kjell—'

'I've got you,' he said as he nudged them closer and closer to the precipice. 'I've got you.'

It was the last thing she heard as they soared together over the edge and into the night sky.

CHAPTER EIGHT

FREYA SIGHED AS she slowly woke. Kjell was watching her from the kitchen, holding a cup of coffee and willing her back to sleep just so he could watch her a little more.

Stalker.

Mm-hmm. He agreed with Enzo's observation. He turned the cup in his hands, missing the man who had been like a brother to him so much that morning it hurt.

What now?

He refused to answer the question that sounded like Enzo, him and even Freya. A Greek chorus commenting on his life. And it was too much, too soon after last night. Another sigh drew his attention back to Freya as she turned beneath the throw he'd had the sanity to cover them with before they'd drifted into sleep just as the sun began to peer through snowflakes that had started to gentle.

His heart thudded in his chest. That she'd

never grow round in pregnancy, that she'd never feel the weight, the child growing within her... He could see how much it devastated her. And he wasn't obtuse. He did understand that she shouldn't have to parade her pain before the world's press and population if she didn't have to. It killed him that he couldn't protect her from that.

But he knew—as much as he wanted to fight it—he instinctively knew that she shouldn't step down. She would lose too much. Her sense of identity was inextricably linked with her role and her place with her family. To lose that as well as the chance to carry a child to term... He shook his head, his heart breaking for her. She wouldn't make it. But he couldn't and wouldn't force that realisation on her. He could only hope to help her understand that for herself.

She stirred again, her body rippling with wakefulness, even though her eyes were still closed.

'Mmm... Coffee?' she asked, turning towards him with a smile. There was a hint of something there in her eyes. Nervousness? Not insecurity, but something...*uncertain*.

In an instant his thoughts and concerns were masked behind a smile, and he allowed some of the wicked heat she inspired in him to show so that doubt disappeared from her gaze.

She reached her arms out from beneath the throw and her body arched into a stretch that threatened to undo his plans. 'Shower.' She exhaled.

'Later. After coffee.'

She frowned.

'I have plans,' he said, answering her unspoken question.

'Plans,' she repeated, desire blooming behind those amber eyes.

He barked a laugh. 'Not *those* kinds of plans.' And he smirked as she pouted.

Freya put her coffee down on the table with a *thunk* as Kjell finished explaining what he had in mind, shock and no small amount of fear shimmering in her chest.

'No! Absolutely not. No. You're insane.'

'It's good for you.'

'There is *nothing* good about that. I'll die. Literally.'

'Don't be silly, you won't die. We do it all the time.'

'Who is this *we*? I don't see anyone else here, and I think you're lying. So, no. I won't do it.'

Kjell laughed again, the sound filling the cabin and warming her chest. It was a glorious sound. Even back at university, she'd not heard it that often and she delighted in hearing it now. Almost enough to give in to his plans. But not quite.

'You'll love it.'

'There is nothing to love about running through a blizzard to a hole in the ice and plunging into literally freezing water. It's dangerous.'

'It's not. I'll be there the whole time. I'll go first, if that makes you feel any better.'

'So what happens after?'

'We come back and shower.'

'There isn't even enough hot water for two of us, Kjell!'

'I've had the generator on and by the time we're back there'll be enough hot water for a whole platoon.'

'Well, good. You and the platoon can make use of it. Because I'm *never* going to do that.'

An hour later, adrenaline buzzed her body and hazed her eyes and for the first time in days it had nothing to do with arousal and everything to do with fear. She could *not* believe that he'd convinced her to do this. He'd left her while he'd found the best place to enter the freezing lake and bashed a hole through the thick icy surface.

'Kjell,' she said, shaking her head and backing away, 'I really can't do this.'

'Of course you can. But it's important that

you do as I do and what I tell you to do.' His tone was level, even and confident. And reasonable. So reasonable that it was *unreasonable*! Her heart was pounding in her chest and her palms kept closing instinctively, as if desperately trying to hold onto something that wasn't there.

She nodded, even though she had no intention of actually following him out to the lake at the bottom of the snow-covered slope and… Her mind stopped short as if trying to protect itself and she couldn't help but laugh at the bubble of hysteria building in her chest.

Dressed in her thermal layers, she was looking out at the lake, which she could now see properly for the first time since the snow had let up. Kjell had promised her the snow would return, the heavy winter storm not quite done with them yet, but here in the blessed calm of the eye of the storm they had a finite amount of time. Time to get to the lake, strip off their clothes while deepening their breathing and facing the cold before plunging into impossibly icy depths. Kjell had staked a rope ladder to the snow-covered bank and she knew it was for her comfort because he'd never need such a thing. The sudden shocking imagined vision of Kjell hauling himself naked from the freezing lake was nearly enough to tempt her into doing as he asked.

And it must have been in a daze of desire that Kjell took her hand and led her out of the cabin because, when she inhaled, the dramatically low temperature stung her lungs and shocked her back into the present, where Kjell was leading her down towards the frozen lake.

'Breathe, Freya,' he ordered, and she did as he asked, and he looked at her with a knowing smile that was as much a taunt as it was reassuring. 'Would I do anything to risk hurting you?' he asked.

Her answer was instantaneous. 'No.'

'And you trust me?'

'Yes.' The response was as instinctive as breathing.

'Move your legs and arms like a warm-up before exercise and deepen your breath.'

Self-consciously, she followed his directions and let her eyes take in the majesty of the surroundings. Rich forest green poked through the white snow, visible through the break in the storm. Deepening her breath, she tasted ice and pine and wildness. All things she would associate with Kjell for ever. Her heart began to slow, but not by much. Especially when Kjell pulled his thermal top over his head and she bit her lip, caging her tongue to stop it from sweeping her lips in delight.

'You scared of it?' he asked, as if unaware of the effect he was having on her right now.

She reluctantly shifted her gaze from the perfection of his chest to the dark, forbidding blackness stark against the snow-covered layer of ice above it. For a moment she wondered if he'd read her mind, asking if she was scared of the feelings building in her hard and fast for a man who, if she stepped down, she could actually have.

'Yes,' she answered, mentally referring to both her feelings and the ice. She didn't have to try to deepen her breath this time, but she slowed it before it could hitch and speed up.

'To face it you need to change the way you think about it. To not see it as a threat, but as an experience. An experience that won't be awful, but incredible.'

His breathing was louder than hers, his wide arms sweeping back and forth, his deep inhalations flaring his nose and just copying his actions was enough to cause adrenaline to rush around her body, for her head to feel light with excitement and challenge. With something that was earthy and elemental and animalistic. Nothing else mattered but them and the frigid water ready to test them, to push them.

To see this terrifying blackness not as something to be feared but as something she could overcome was incredible.

Kjell's words were hypnotic, calling to something fierce within her, the sister of yesterday's rage and hurt, but this time more determined, exhilarating. Something that revelled at being on the brink of an act both terrifying and suddenly absolutely necessary to her. She needed to do this. She felt it in her soul and as strongly as she needed her next breath. And Kjell smiled as if sensing that change in her.

'Do you want to go first?'

She nodded, unable to open her jaw, it was clenched in fear and determination.

'Breathe. Relax into it. Be bold and brave and you will conquer it.'

She forced her body to submit to the world around her as she stripped off her layers, toeing off the boots he'd lent her and down to her underwear.

'You can take those off too,' he taunted, and she laughed out loud, the action cutting through some of the tension.

She stood there for a moment, breathing deep, her hopes and fears warring for mastery of her body.

'Remember. Go slowly and use the rope.'

He'd told her that the lake wasn't deep here,

that she'd easily reach the bottom, but she clung to that rope with white knuckles as she stepped into the dark abyss, breathing through the impulse to cry her shock out loud.

It was so cold that at first she felt nothing. But her body had reacted even if her nerves were still playing catch-up. She gasped for breath, fighting the need to tense, but it was the adrenaline that shocked her the most. She inhaled and wanted to laugh. Wanted to scream into the air around them. As sensation began to bleed into her skin, an inconceivable coldness drenched her. Her body was alive and bursting with something indescribable, her heart pounding, not from fear but from vitality, from life. From the utter shock that she was there, in the freezing cold, breathing through her body's reaction to the impossibly cold water.

Kjell joined her, his gaze locked on hers as if delighting in nothing more than simply her experience of this gift he'd given her. Because it was a gift. She'd spent so long feeling numb after her diagnosis. Numb to her body's failings and absence. *This* was something her body *could* do. The miraculous abilities that she still had within her.

She reached for him and drew him in to a kiss, powerful, demanding as their tongues clashed and tasted and tested and revelled.

He slowed the kiss, as if reluctant, just as she began to feel her foot curl into what could soon be a cramp.

'That's probably enough for today,' he said, as if knowing her limits better than she. Freya would have protested, but actually her bones were beginning to ache from the cold. Kjell hauled himself out from the hole he'd dug in the ice and turned, his black trunks plastered to his skin, outlining every delicious inch of him and the powerful thighs that braced as he gave her his hand and pulled her from the ice water as if she weighed nothing. In an instant her teeth began to chatter and he wrapped a warm blanket around her, rubbing at her skin, less to dry and more to warm.

'You are incredible,' he said with a pride that stole her heart. And with that he lifted her in his arms, marched them back to the cabin and together they showered for a *very* long time.

Kjell placed a bottle of wine on the table, promising himself that, no matter how bad dinner might be, he would eat it. Freya had been a terrible cook at university, he doubted that she'd had much practice since.

There had been something seductively domestic about the afternoon. The snow had resumed almost immediately upon their return to the cabin—as if the pause in the weather had been just for them. The fire had blazed in the burner, Freya had teased a book from the shelves and curled up beside him before falling asleep on his shoulder. She'd been so deeply under that he'd turned lengthways on the sofa and pulled her gently up against him, cradling her with his body. And he'd done nothing but relish every second of it.

He'd felt a peace he'd not experienced for years and hoarded it within him for the years to come after she returned to her royal duties. Even if she couldn't see a way, Kjell would find one. Because it was in her blood, she'd been born to it. And he knew in his bones how damaging not doing the one thing you lived and breathed for could be.

'Ta-da!' Freya said, placing the pan on the table mat, tendrils of smoke escaping from the burnt edges of the pan.

'Smells...delightful,' he said, his voice high-pitched even to his own ears. She looked up at him, eyes wide but hopeful. He picked up a spoon from the table and plunged it into the mysteriously beige depths of the pan. 'What is it?' he asked hesitantly.

'You tell me.'

'Oka-ay,' he said, the word broken by his concern. He put the spoon into his mouth and just barely managed to stop himself from spitting it back out. 'It's...um...' He looked at her and swallowed. 'You don't know what it is, do you?' he accused.

'Not really. Is it...*edible*?'

He barked out a laugh. 'You haven't even tried it?'

'God, no. It smells awful.'

He'd forgotten this side of her. The playful, fun, teasing side to her. He wondered if she had too, from the way that the light sparkled in her eyes.

'You could teach me, you know,' she said, removing the pan as he entered the kitchen space to pull together a half decent meal. Thankfully, the bread was still fresh and would certainly work with smoked fish, pâtés, pickles, cheeses and smoked meat.

'Teach you what?' he asked, distracted, setting the rye bread to toast.

'To cook.'

His actions slowed as he caught the tone of her voice. 'That could take a while,' he replied cautiously.

'It will take *years*, Kjell.'

He clamped his jaw shut, turning back to the table to pour them some wine, his fingers white-knuckled around the green glass bottle. He knew what she was doing. Building a dream around a future that wasn't possible. He'd done it himself and had been devastated when that dream disintegrated. So devastated that he'd agreed to every single UN overseas mission possible. He'd stayed away from his family, from his country and anything that had reminded him of her.

And, despite that pain, he still wanted to give in to the picture she was painting, to get even just a glimpse of a future in which there was no throne, no active service, just them. The ache of knowing how perfect it would be was worth the agony of it being taken away. Because in that moment, for just a heartbeat, they'd been together, imagining the same future. But he'd stopped lying the day he'd last seen her eight years ago. To others. To himself.

'Freya,' he said, turning towards her.

'And I was thinking,' she pressed on, ignoring him, ignoring the warning in his tone. 'Perhaps I could come here? You know. After I step down from my title. It's just so peaceful here. And I'd *love* to see it in the summer. I imagine that it's stunning. Is it? Stunning?'

She was rambling, clinging to this fantasy with desperate fingers. It was there in her eyes. *Please. Please let me have this.*

He heard it as clear as if she'd said it. His heart turned over. There was time. The storm still raged and there was *still* time, he promised himself. He looked up at her, knowing that he'd never be able to deny her anything.

'It's absolutely breathtaking,' he said. 'The sun's rays filter through the trees and in the early morning, as the earth warms, before the rest of the world wakes, it's like heaven on earth.'

'I want to see that one day.'

'Then you shall.'

He placed the meal he'd cobbled together on two large chopping boards on the table. Cool white wine filled large old glasses, the condensation forming against the warmth of the room from the wood burner.

'Forget what I said about learning to cook. I'm never cooking. Dinner will be on you every night,' she said, her eyes large and hungry looking at the food and he smiled in spite of himself.

'So what will you do?' he asked, hypothetically playing along for the moment.

'Probably something in the charity sector. It's what I love doing most.'

'What are you currently working on?' he asked, subtly leading her back to her current role. Her eyes were bright and her cheeks pink, this time there was no rambling. Just pure confidence and joy in her work, at what she helped achieve.

'I'm trying to get Stellan Stormare in front of parliament, but they're still resistant to it.'

'The man whose daughter died?'

Freya nodded. 'Lena Stormare was on a train filled with hundreds of people and not one of them knew sign language, not one of them was able to help her in time.' Freya's fury was simmering bright in her eyes but, rather than overwhelming her like it had yesterday, it empowered her, gave her something that few others were capable of. 'She died from an allergic reaction and couldn't tell anyone.' She shook her head, the loss clearly a burden on her heart. 'I don't understand why we're not teaching it in our schools.'

'You could argue that funding should go where there is the greatest need.'

'And what greater need is there than to be able to communicate?'

He raised his hands. 'I'm playing devil's advocate.'

'Yes, I know the arguments—there are fewer children with hearing difficulties, there are more worthy or urgent causes. But why do people think that it only benefits the young? What about the elderly with hearing loss? If sign language was learned by the many, used regularly, then I *know* it would be beneficial there too. In this day and age shouldn't we be doing everything we can to ensure we can *all* speak and we can *all* be heard?' Her passion made her fierce—worthy and admirable. He wished she could see what he saw. Someone ready, willing, able and more than capable to fight for those who could not fight for themselves. But why couldn't she fight for *herself* with that same passion?

'What about Aleksander? Surely your brother can help?'

'He's got enough on his plate at the moment.'

'It can't be easy,' he said truthfully. As Lieutenant Colonel, he knew what it was like to lead hundreds, if not thousands of people. He also knew what it was like to be tied to a course of action he knew in his gut was wrong but was helpless to change. Whether Aleksander's hands were tied by royal statutes or political gambles, it was hard to make changes when all were against it.

'Will you be able to help Stellan before you step down?' he asked, knowing instantly that he'd found a weak spot in her plan. If he was on the attack, if he truly wanted to hit home, this would be the way to do it. It was a low blow, but it was for her. Always for her.

'I will do everything in my power before then and after if need be.'

Of course—they were both ignoring Aleksander's stipulation. That in order for Freya to step down, he would need to accept the medal. His gut clenched with the suspicion that Aleksander had done this on purpose. It would have been a win/win for Aleksander; either he expected Kjell to convince her not to step down, or Freya to convince him to take the medal.

The crisp bread dried on his tongue, leaching moisture from his mouth, parching his lips and throat and he reached for his wine. Everything in him roared in denial. The food turned sour in his stomach. How could he accept a medal for the mission that had put Enzo in the ground? No. It wasn't the mission that had put him in the ground. It had been Kjell.

Freya noticed the change in him almost immediately. It was a stillness. A retreat. He filled her glass and peppered her with questions about what kind of help Stellan's cause might need in the long-term, but it was as if Kjell wasn't really there. For a man who had been so truly focused on her since the moment she'd arrived it was a stark absence—and one that she knew was deeply enmeshed with the AAR and the medal.

A medal he would have to accept if she were to actually be allowed to step down.

She hated that her freedom would come at

such a cost to him. It silenced the question every time it lay on her tongue. Kjell was the most dedicated, determined man she knew. Time hadn't changed that—in fact, it seemed to have only made him more so. It was one of the things that she had admired about him, that connected them on a fundamental level: a sense of duty. That he had respected hers, understood it rather than questioning or resenting it had made him even more precious to her. And it was also why she knew that something truly awful must have happened to affect him so. But it was hidden behind a wall of silence, a wall that could damage as well as protect.

Freya looked out of the window. The interior light picked out a few flakes as they twisted and fell across a nightscape dark and forbidding. The wood burner was glowing with heat and she should have felt cosy, but the chill from Kjell was as brutal as the shocking cold water she'd plunged into today.

'Coffee?' Kjell's question interrupted her thoughts. She looked down at her plate and found it empty and nodded as he picked it up and took the rest of the things to the kitchen.

'Yes please,' she answered, wondering how to even begin to approach such a difficult subject. He had teased a confession from her with sensual delight and pleasure—but that wouldn't work for him. The soldier in him wouldn't appreciate anything less than a direct confrontation, but she felt deep in her bones that it wasn't the soldier she needed to reach.

She heard him fill the percolator and couldn't sit still. Standing up, she went to him, unable to resist the need to reach out to him, to forge the connection his retreat complicated. Freya wrapped her arms around him from behind and placed her cheek against his back, comforted by the steady pulse of his heart and warmed by his body. He tensed, as if caught by surprise, his muscles rigid before he gave in, his body relaxing within hers as he placed his hand on top of hers, holding them there in that moment.

'Please don't.' His voice was quiet but raw, knowing the question on her tongue.

She closed her eyes, hating that she couldn't let this go. But it was no longer about whether he took the medal or not, this was about so much more. He needed to face whatever it was that was ravaging his soul.

'Will you tell me what happened?'

CHAPTER NINE

KJELL GRIPPED THE handle of the percolator with white knuckles, thankful that Freya was tucked behind him and not witnessing his reaction to her question. He considered it. Refusing her. For the first time in his life, he actually *wanted* to deny her.

Anger and fear were bitter on his tongue. 'I can't help you, Princess,' he said, taking the bubbling, spitting percolator from the stove. 'I'd take the medal in a heartbeat if I thought it was the right thing for you, but I don't,' he said honestly. 'So I won't.'

She held onto him, despite his small movements and his harsh words. Her arms were loose but strong. Determined but with a softness that somehow reminded him of a comfort he hadn't known in years. His heart pulsed beneath the touch.

'I won't be distracted, Kjell.' Her tone patient, calm, *kind*.

'It doesn't mean it's not true.'

'Neither does it make it an answer to my question.' Again, her gentleness. If she'd come at him with commands and orders, he'd have been able to fight her. But she hadn't. Whether she knew it or not, it was this, her natural empathetic will to understand that made her the perfect princess. He inhaled, the scent of rich coffee invading his senses, but in his mind he could smell cheap instant granules, thick as syrup and foul as earth.

It's the only way to drink it, mio amico.

Enzo's laugh melded with the piercing rumble of the IED explosion and his heart thumped, a cold sweat threatening to break out at the back of his neck. He clenched his teeth, trying to ground himself in the present.

But that wasn't what brought him back. He looked down to find Freya's fingers slipping through the spaces between his own, her palm over his hand, light, warm but more of an anchor than any he'd ever felt.

You trust me?

Yes.

The gift of her trust, after their past but also because of it, meant she deserved nothing less than the same in return. He'd not spoken of it once in the last four months. He'd not been able to. But now, with Freya, the words, the thoughts, they were clamouring to get out. As if they'd been waiting only for her. He turned to find her looking up at him, warm whisky-coloured eyes patient and open.

'Go sit down,' she said, nodding back towards the large sofa, clearly having sensed his decision. 'I'll bring the coffee.'

He picked up their joined hands and pressed a kiss to her knuckles before releasing their hold and heading to the sofa on feet that left imprints in sand. Already his mind was back there, straddling the past and the present. He could feel the sweat dripping down his spine, soaking his T-shirt and chest, and was half convinced that if he wiped at his forehead his wrist would come back slick and salty.

He swallowed around an arid heat that sucked any and all moisture from his body. Over the sounds of coffee being poured, he heard the sound of children's laughter. A beautiful chatter clashing with the tinkle of a spoon against ceramic.

And Enzo, laughing like the biggest kid in the playground, kicking the football into the square in the sand that marked the goal.

Freya pressed a hot mug into his hands before pulling up the foot stool so she could sit opposite him. Within touching distance—if he wanted—but also giving him space.

'Where were you stationed?'

He shook his head gently. 'It doesn't really matter. We're stationed wherever violence meets the shift of power. It could have been anywhere around the world,' he said with a finality he felt to the bottom of his heart. That man's ability to cause great acts of violence in the name of both justice and injustice didn't surprise him any more should have been warning enough.

'We were there to facilitate the transition of political power, but also for DDR.'

'Disarmament, demobilisation and reintegration?'

Kjell nodded. 'Some of these guys, they've been fighting since they were just kids. It's all they know. And when the peace process begins there's no job to walk into, there's no place in society for them, because they've been on the outside with no way back. It's as important to bring them back into their community as it is to disarm. Training, education options, ways for them to contribute to society—if peace isn't people-centred, then it has no hope.'

Kjell had seen it time and time again in the last eight years. The need to work *with* a community, to support, facilitate, enable rather than lead, dominate, overpower. That was peacekeeping at its best. That, to him, was a duty with the highest of callings.

'I was responsible for nearly six hundred soldiers.'

'How many are deployed?'

'In that region? About eleven thousand.'

She seemed surprised. 'Do the units stay the same?' she asked.

'People circulate. Most do their secondments and return home. Others…' He shrugged. Even now, as he looked back he could recognise that he'd had a choice. He could have challenged the exile. In fact, his commanding officer in the Svardian Armén had been trying to get him back on home soil for at least two years now. 'We come from all around the world—each member state contributing certain numbers if and where they can,' he explained.

'Some of you stay?'

'When we can.'

'Do you want to go back?' she asked hesitantly.

He didn't know if he could. Not now. Not after. And that thought alone cost him greatly. He looked across the room to the stack of paperwork Freya had pushed to the side and saw the AAR on the top. The report, nearly two weeks overdue now. A year ago such a thing would have been inconceivable.

'I'd known Enzo for about five years. We'd crossed over on a number of missions in a number of different locations. He was all Italian charm. Quick with a joke, a leer and a laugh. But he loved his wife,' Kjell said with the first sincere smile she'd seen lift his lips since dinner. 'At least once a day we'd be subjected to rhapsodies about her beauty and her kindness. He gloried in his love for her,' he said, Kjell's tone full of amusement. 'The sonnets he could have written about her hair alone...' He half laughed, and Freya felt her lips curve into a smile.

Kjell leaned his head on his hand, elbow rested on knee and eyes locked on somewhere Freya would never likely see, remembering someone she would never meet. Her heart ached, instinctively knowing the end to this story and wishing there could be another way for Kjell to face his demons.

'We were at the end of our patrol. We should have been heading back to base, but we were rerouted.'

There was something about the way he said that last bit, a shift in tone that didn't sit right.

'You disagreed with the command?'

'I would never disobey a direct order.' Grim-lipped and pale, Kjell's eyes were locked on a distant horizon.

Freya frowned, trying to find the right words. 'Did you question it?'

His jaw flexed, the muscle tight and his skin flushed with anger. 'No.'

Oh. Her heart ached for him. She could see it now. He had disagreed with the order but, as a dutiful and conscientious soldier, couldn't, *wouldn't*, question it.

'Chain of command is just as important on the ground for UN missions as it is with any other deployed army,' he ground out through teeth clenched so hard she feared something might break.

She placed her hand on his forearm, but he didn't seem to notice.

'But I could feel it,' he said, his unseeing gaze finally clearing enough to lock onto hers. 'In my gut. We both did. We both knew it was wrong. We were to help safeguard a group of foreign nationals who had gone off-itinerary to visit a local community centre. The intention was good enough, but the security plan wasn't in place to cover it and they clearly didn't realise how unstable the region was. Absolutely they needed the support, but there were two other patrols who were fresher and just as close.'

'So why were you sent?'

Kjell's eyes shifted from dusk to midnight in a heartbeat. 'They were showing off. They wanted to send *me*,' he said, jerking a thumb back into his chest, 'a high-ranking senior officer.'

Freya felt her eyes grow wide and round. The agony in his tone, the bitterness and hurt, was awful for her to hear.

'We all knew it. Showboating for the oil execs. The squad shared eye-rolls and friendly banter, but I didn't like it. It was *wrong*.'

'Kjell—' She wanted to tell him he could stop, wanted to protect him from reliving such great pain, but it was as if he couldn't hear her.

'When we got there, the visit from the oil execs had drawn a lot of unwanted attention and a crowd was beginning to form. Some of the young teenagers at the community centre had been part of the reintegration programme, having turned their backs on the local militia. Most of these boys, Freya—they'd been taken when they were five or six…and at sixteen they were still fighting for their freedom.'

Her heart ached for children she would never meet, their struggle as impossible and inconceivable to her as it was an anathema.

'Foreign execs and ex-child soldiers. It was exactly the kind of target that the militia liked best. We were on the radio before the convoy could pull to a stop, calling for reinforcements.'

Freya wondered what he saw in his mind—his gaze fixed over her shoulder.

'They were probably already there—the rogue militia, indistinguishable from the people in the crowd who had gathered to support the centre or had been drawn there by curiosity about the visitors.'

The weight of eyes on the back of his neck lifted the hairs on his arms. They'd all felt it, each member of his team, the way that the crowd's energy changed like a discordant note rippling through a piece of music, changing the tone irrevocably.

'The glass bottle, thrown near the steps of the centre, was just a test.'

The glass had shattered suddenly on the dry ground, but a community ravaged by decades of violence and tension needed barely a spark. They knew what was coming. Screams echoed in his ears as hundreds of people scattered into chaos, making it impossible to identify where the threat was. The unit spread out, each soldier knowing their individual role. Four of his team took up defensive positions around the execs and students in the community centre, while Enzo and six others spread out into the seething mass of the crowd.

One shot. Then two, then three, the tattoo sounding his ears. The dry wood of the community centre shattered and splintered around the bullets.

'There were at least two enemy combatants

in the crowd, but a third holed-up in one of the buildings off the square was pinning down a small section of the civilians Enzo and the others had managed to corral behind some of the market stalls.'

He'd caught Enzo's eye across the chaos, gesturing sharply with his hand, the communication clear, but not to the other man's liking. They never went off alone, but there wasn't time to debate. He repositioned himself and when Enzo lay down covering fire, Kjell slipped out from behind the vehicle and covered the space between him and the corner building in a heartbeat and a prayer. Training kicked in—clearing the entrance, the first room, the second and into the stairwell he knew would lead up to the third man.

Enzo and the rest of his team would handle the two rogue militia that had lodged themselves into positions in the marketplace, of that he had no doubt. But the civilians in the square had no chance with this man in the equation. Backup was far enough away for him to pick them off one by one. On silent feet, Kjell timed his steps with the gunshots coming from the room one floor above to his right.

'You killed him,' Freya said, a statement rather than a question.

'It took me seven of his bullets to traverse

two floors and get him in my sights. Seven bullets that wounded two women, three teenage boys, and killed one child and one man. A man who had used his body to shield six young children who had been on a day trip with their class to the community centre.'

From the corner of his eye he saw Freya press a shaking hand to her lips, but in his heart he saw dust and blood.

'Enzo died instantly, protecting children who survived with nothing more than cuts and bruises.' Backup had arrived, the oil execs were rushed into waiting vehicles, while he and his team… It had been a terrible thing to be united in. A shared moment of horror. And then training and duty had kicked in, the area split into quadrants and searched for any sign of the rebel militia. His team had stayed in the market square, guarding the injured until the medics arrived.

Guarding the dead.

Freya's breath hitched, drawing his gaze to hers, the haunting pale amber of her eyes filled with a sorrow so pure he was humbled by it. She anchored him back in the present, picking up his hand and placing it over a heart that beat for him, the rhythm stuttering, hurt and somehow matching his own. He closed his eyes, savouring the moment, the feeling. The comfort she gave allowed grief to fill the spaces in his heart that had been consumed with such *anger*.

He fisted his hand, remembering his return to base. 'I was called in to discuss the fallout,' he said bitterly. 'It was just me and the top brass.' He shook his head, biting down, hearing again the way the situation had been presented to him. 'Everything that was reported …the order, it was all perfectly correct. But…' He steeled himself, his body flexing, his shoulders squaring and his back straightening. 'I am a *good* soldier. Dutiful. I *believe* in the mission. I believe in the chain of command. I understand it. But I'm not sure that I…trust it any more. And if I can't do that…'

He shook his head, unwilling and unable to follow that thought to its logical conclusion. It wasn't just a job for him. It was an identity; his units, his placements, they'd become his family, his home.

'I haven't questioned a command since—' He snapped his teeth together.

'Since me?' she asked, her eyes glowing in the dim lighting of the cabin. His answer was in his eyes. She seemed not to need more than that. 'What is stopping you from writing the AAR?' she asked gently.

'I can't see the situation dispassionately. I can't outline the events without bias, without anger, without the clarity to know whether what happened could have had a different outcome, because every time I think about it, it makes me question everything I know. Everything I've given up for this job, this life.' It was the first time he'd finally said it out loud. Finally put his fear into words that explained, that made coherence from the chaos of his feelings. 'I don't know whether command made the right call. I don't know whether they should have sent another unit, I don't know whether I should have waited... I just... Enzo was...'

He hated that the words he needed to say were getting caught in his throat. That he couldn't speak for his friend, for himself.

'Enzo was a hero.' Freya's reverent voice slipped around his soul.

'Yes, he was,' he said, refusing to acknowledge the dampness pressing against his eyes. 'But,' he said, turning to Freya, '*I* am not. So your brother can keep his damn medal.'

He stood up before he could betray himself any more and went to step away when he felt Freya's hand sneak around his thigh, gently holding him in place better than any restraint could have ever done.

'What would have happened if you hadn't gone after the third man?'

'What?'

'If you'd not been there to do what you did?'

He looked down at her, unable to lie. It would have been a massacre. He didn't need to say it to know that she heard his silent response.

Freya let him leave. She knew he needed time and space, but was worried when she heard the door to the outside open and close. Looking through the window, she was surprised to see that the snow had stopped again. Clouds still blanketed the sky, airbrushing the finer details from the view.

Her inhalation was shaky from the way her heart still trembled for him. Kjell's pain and grief for his friend was beyond anything she knew or had experienced. She could only hope that talking about it had drawn the poisonous pain from his soul.

But even if she had helped him somehow, she knew that the damage had been done. In his exile, Kjell had found a family and found a place he could lay his head. But Enzo's death had changed that for him. Once again, his family, his support, had been stolen from him.

She had believed him when he said he'd had cause to question his decisions, his job, himself. And she knew how that could be—how painful, disruptive...how damaging. But, oh, she wished he could see what she saw when she looked at him.

A conscientious soldier who thought about the impact of his actions. Who cared about the people under his protection in the present as much as in the future. A man whose moral compass was so strong he had punished himself for the lie of a boy bound in duty to a king, long into his adulthood.

A man who she had never stopped loving. In all those years, it had been there. Him. In her heart.

And a man who she could absolutely have for herself if she walked away from the throne. She didn't need Aleksander's permission. Not really. It had been a lie that she'd told herself, because it gave the power to someone else to decide her fate. Because she couldn't trust herself to choose correctly. She knew that walking away from her title would be best for her brother, her sister, the royal family. But would it be best for Svardia?

Her heart in turmoil, she finally heard what Kjell had been trying to tell her. That yes, she could walk away, she could find true happiness with the man she loved. Or she could return to Svardia and stay, do something real and good with her life and her time for the people of her country, for women all across the world. She could give them a voice, just as she'd wished for Lena Stormare.

But it would cost her Kjell.

Earlier, over dinner, she'd woven a fantasy that was so pure it hurt too much to want it. Behind her closed eyes, Kjell chopped wood in the sunshine. Bees buzzed and butterflies zigzagged across the meadow outside. The windows were thrown open to let warm summer air into the cabin and the sounds of children's laughter danced on the breeze.

And she opened her eyes to release tears that stung as they fell. Loss. Grief. For what could never be. This. This was more of a loss than a crown or a title. And it was a loss and a grief that she refused to tie Kjell to. He deserved a home. And children of his own. A whole platoon of them to order around, to teach...to love. She couldn't bind him to anything less than that. He would—she knew—sacrifice anything for her and she could not, would not, do that to him again.

Kjell watched the night sky as the thick bank of clouds began to shift beneath strong winds. He wondered if they were working their magic on him too, or whether that was Freya. She had always hit him like a tornado. A storm, swirling him up in its eye, as if she were the centre of everything, grounding him, focusing him.

His muscles hurt as if he'd just finished a particularly brutal workout—the tension becoming acidic the moment he gave up the fight of holding everything in. His heart ached for Enzo and guilt at not being able to save him stabbed his conscience. But for the first time since that awful day he felt that he could breathe a little easier, that his anger was just a little less.

Fury and grief had been so huge in his mind and his heart, he'd not known whether he'd still be standing when the tide of words washed through those feelings. But Freya had been there to anchor him. Not to hold him in place, but to come back to. A tether he'd needed in order to face those fears, to survive them.

He'd come out here, not because he needed to be alone but because if he'd stayed he would have said the words carved into his heart so many years ago. And if he spoke them he knew that it would make it harder for her to leave. And no matter how much he loved her, how much he desperately wanted the future she'd painted over dinner, he knew that it was not *her* future.

She had been born to be Svardia's Princess. More so than any other member of her family.

The faith and love she had in and for her people, *all* her people, was the true jewel of the crown. And he couldn't let her sacrifice that. Not from fear. Not when he knew, he *knew*, she had the strength and determination to face down anything that was thrown at her. That she would be integral to turn the tide in attitudes, to ensure a greater understanding and, even more, that she could be an advocate for that change.

Deep within him was a conviction so sure, so strong, that she would achieve truly great things. Pride, fierce and powerful, rippled through him at the thought. She was already magnificent in his eyes. He just couldn't wait for the world to see it too. Even if it meant he could never be by her side. Even if it meant that he'd never get to tease her about her cooking, or argue with her views, kiss away her anger or soothe her hurts. Even if it meant that he could never tell her that he loved her.

He heard the crunch of her boots in the snow behind him and he turned, not wanting to miss a single second of the little time they had left together. Shapeless in the thick outdoor jacket, hat, boots and scarf, Freya had never looked more beautiful to him. Her eyes gleamed as the last of the clouds passed from the sky to reveal the scattering of diamonds against velvet above them and still the majesty of the natural world wasn't enough to draw his gaze from her.

She looked as if she were about to say something when her eyes locked on something over his shoulder and widened in awe as a gasp fell from her lips and even then he couldn't look away from her. He imagined what she was seeing. Invisible until the thick heavy clouds passed from the sky, the northern lights bathed the stars in colours that seemed unnatural. Her eyes danced across the twists and turns of a kaleidoscope, focusing in and out on a whole palette of incandescent greens, purples, pinks and more.

'It's incredible,' she said, the words dropping from her lips in whispered awe.

'It is,' he agreed, thinking only of her, his heart stuttering over a beat when she moved her gaze from the sky to his.

'How long do you think we have?' she asked, and he was unable and unwilling to pretend not to know what she meant.

'They'll probably arrive a few hours after dawn.'

She nodded, something passing across her gaze before she blinked it away.

'I'll take the medal.' The words rushed out of him but he wouldn't take them back. It was the only thing he could give her. She smiled then. It was sad but strong, hurt but alive, and then it was his turn to smile.

It killed him, tore his heart in two, but he wouldn't have it any other way. 'You're going to keep your title. You're going to stay a princess.'

He lifted his hand to cup her jaw and she nodded into his palm, turning her lips to press sad kisses that mixed with the single tear that escaped across her cheek.

'I can't say goodbye. Not yet. Please don't make me say it.' She spoke into his hand, her eyes pressed closed as if in denial of what was happening.

'Then we won't,' he said simply as if his heart hadn't fractured a thousand times over.

CHAPTER TEN

FLAMES FLICKERED FROM the wood burner in the dark cabin; the light left off from when she had gone to find Kjell by the lake. She went to the switch but he stopped her, taking her hand in his and leading her to the window, where the entire landscape was a glowing display of vibrant colours that burned her heart.

She would never see this again. Not from this cabin, not from beside this man. He stood behind her and she felt so safe. So protected. But she knew that she couldn't have him. She loved him but, for the first time in her life, she thought that it wasn't enough.

'Make me forget. Just for tonight?' she whispered into the room. From behind her, he placed a kiss on her shoulder, then her neck, then that secret place that sent shivers down her spine and across her stomach. She spun in his arms to face him, to see him for as long as possible, even if they only had hours left. Her hands reached for his face, drawing him towards her, and she curved into him as his lips took hers. Tongues thrust and parried, teeth nipped and teased, hearts pounded and pulses tripped.

She couldn't get enough, touch enough, taste enough. She wanted to consume a lifetime's worth of him and still it wouldn't be enough. His skin was hot and smooth beneath her palms, her fingers inching beneath the jumper, sweeping up over muscles that rippled beneath her hands, and she wanted it against her own.

She tugged at his jumper impatiently, pulling and pushing, but not managing either, until his hands swept hers aside and he drew the jumper over his head, cast it aside and returned to a kiss that had her toes curling. It should have been funny, but it wasn't. It was sad and she wanted to cry and the kisses weren't enough and the need she felt would never be sated. The hurt she felt would never be healed. She gasped into his kiss, grief a hitch in her breath, the feeling of loss too soon and too much.

His kiss gentled and became soothing and reassuring as if trying to calm the ferocious hurt that swept over her. His palm was hot against her back, his fingers toying with the hem of her top, but it wasn't enough, not nearly. She pulled the top over her head and, like he had, cast it aside. She'd not worn a bra that morning and his eyes feasted on her, roaming her flame-licked skin as if imprinting it on his mind for years to come.

He reached up, palming her breasts at the same time, the warmth, the possessiveness of his touch, the way his thumbs toyed with her nipples bringing fissures of pleasure to a shell she'd not realised she'd worn ever since the night they'd parted eight years ago. It shattered beneath his touch, exposing the vulnerable untouched heart of her. She wanted to give him this. He deserved that much at least. If this night—this stolen night—was all they were to have then they would make enough memories for them both to last a lifetime.

Her determination made her bold. She pulled him back to her, this time *her* lips, her touch possessive and needy. She had been consumed by him once. Now she wanted to consume. Her tongue thrust deep into his mouth, his eyes flaring at the invasion, the primal claim she laid against him. Her fingers rifling through the thick golden strands and framing his head as she pressed herself up against his chest, delighting in the friction of his skin against her already taut nipples. His hand swept down and around her backside, squeezing her against him and pressing the length of his arousal against her core. Through the layers of clothing she felt him, felt his heat, his need for her and she wanted it, she wanted it all.

He drew her thigh upwards, hooking her leg over his hip, the angle a heavenly pressure on the sensitive bundle of nerves at the heart of her need and she cried out into his mouth. Shivering, her fingers flew to his trousers, freeing the button and pulling at the tab of the zip, but before she could draw it down he hoisted her up into his arms and she was forced to wrap her other leg around him for stability.

'You're rushing me,' he growled against her mouth.

She held back a smile. 'I am not. I'm rushing *me*.'

'There's no need. I'm going to take my time with you.'

'Actually,' she replied archly, 'I had planned to take my time with—'

He dropped down to the sofa, cradling her in his lap, but shocking the breath from her lungs and hauling her up against his chest. His hand palmed her backside, long fingers inching further beneath her, sensual anticipation driving her wild. She lifted to give him more room, arching into him, her breasts pressing against his chest, her breath expanding in her lungs, wanting, needing. But an arched brow above a knowing gaze pressed her back down and Freya knew she was being toyed with. Perhaps, Freya thought wryly, he had forgotten who he was playing with.

Having Freya hot and wanting in his lap was a lifetime of fantasies rolled into one. She twisted and turned like flames in his grasp, but if this was the last night they would share together he wanted to savour every minute of it. And he wasn't above teasing her to get what he wanted. He pulled gently on her shoulders, pressing her into his lap and sending her head backwards, the pleasure she found there shivering across her skin, but by the time she raised her head to look at him, wickedness sparked in her gaze and he stilled for long enough to wonder what she had planned. That second was, apparently, all she needed.

Placing her hands on his thighs, she lifted herself off his lap and slid between his legs. It was so quick he'd not been able to catch her and, before he could move, she'd undone the zip of his trousers and his heart was pounding so hard in his chest he thought he'd be able to see it.

'Freya...' It was supposed to have been an admonishment, but instead it came out half plea, half prayer and all curse. He wouldn't last. Not like this. Not even in his wildest fantasies had he seen his princess on her knees before him and just the sight of it was enough to undo him.

And he didn't doubt for one second that she knew it too. He reached for where her hands sat at the top of his thighs and she batted him away. Clenching his jaw, he pressed his fists down on the sofa cushion beside his legs and watched her like a hawk. The curve to her lip was victorious and he wouldn't do anything to take that away from her. It made his heart soar. Until it stopped altogether as her eyes widened to the size of saucers when she realised he wasn't wearing anything beneath his trousers.

Pressing apart the trouser opening, she reached for him and he flinched, his erection jerking against her palm in arousal and need. His fist tightened on itself, pressing deeper and harder into the cushion as he held himself back.

Her fingers wrapped around him, flexing against his hardened length, drawing her caress upwards, slowly, *so* slowly, before gliding down and, before he could think to stop her, she took him into her mouth and he turned the air blue with curses that would have shocked even his soldiers.

He pressed his fisted hand against his mouth

to prevent anything further escaping—like the groan that was building in the back of his throat and the pleas that were threatening to undo any semblance of manhood he'd ever had. Begging was not an option.

At least not until she swirled her tongue around the delicate head of his penis and he knew he was going to hell.

The thrill of holding him in her mouth was something Freya could never have imagined. The power and trust of it humbled her. But it was the pleasure she took from it for herself that was the surprise. Skin like smooth velvet wrapped around steel that she couldn't get enough of. She took him in further and deeper until he filled her mouth completely and she didn't think she could take any more. But the sound of the growl Kjell made, primal and desperate, and all the things he made her feel... it made her wet with want. Her eyes flickered up to his and she froze.

The sheer ferocity of need in his eyes had her heart tripping over itself. The low pulse that had throbbed incessantly now stung with the intensity of arousal flickering over her skin and in the hollow of her body that wanted nothing more than him to fill it. She thought she'd felt empty before, when she'd received her diagnosis. But the *force* she wanted him with… she would never feel complete without him.

In that moment before she could properly understand her own thoughts he claimed back control, gently pulling her up, both of them slick with want and need. He wasted no time in peeling the thermal layers away from her waist, down her hips and from her legs, one at a time. And just like that she was naked in his lap, the rough feel of his trouser zip on the underside of her sensitive thighs sending shivers through her body.

She shifted in his lap, teasing herself against the hardened length of him, and when she saw him watching her she blushed.

'Don't stop.' The rough words sounding ripped from him.

'What?' she asked, avoiding the fierce heat of his gaze.

'Never stop taking your pleasure,' he commanded, his eyes dark with desire and something that looked almost like desperation. 'There is *nothing* more beautiful to see than you taking your pleasure from me.'

She speared her bottom lip with her teeth, as both an anchor and a bloom of infinitesimal hurt to keep the need coursing through her veins in check. She was breathless with want—the look in his eyes a challenge, a *dare*.

What do you need to believe again?

He was showing her how much of a woman she was—whether she could have children or not. Whether they had a future together or not—he was giving her this. He was showing her how to take her power.

She rolled her hips, sliding against the hard length of him, the sweep across her clitoris sensual, slick and violently arousing. It came on fast—the waves of desire washing through her body, building and building, sighs and groans hitching her breath higher and higher. Before her mind could process the incredible sensation, Kjell gripped her hips, adding his hold to the pressure and her back bowed as she came, her eyes saw stars as Kjell worshipped her breasts, his hold on her safe and protective.

Freya returned to the feel of Kjell's arms around her, holding her upright in his lap, pressing delicate kisses to her collarbone that threatened to reignite a fire only just tempered.

'Stay with me,' he said between kisses. 'Don't return to Svardia.' Her heart twisted at his words, her soul aching to say yes. Openmouthed, he kissed down to her shoulder and back, his tongue teasing and teeth gently marking. 'We can spend the rest of our days making love in front of the fire, watching the seasons change, the sun rise and set before the northern lights, and eat absolutely none of your cooking,' he said and she could feel the smile on his lips against her skin. 'Stay with me,' he whispered.

It was a call she felt to the depth of her soul. She wanted it so much it hurt to breathe.

'Kjell…'

'I know. I know I shouldn't ask, and I know even more that you shouldn't stay here. You need to be the Princess you were born to be. I would never take that away from you. I just… I need a minute to be selfish before I let you go.'

It was those things, but it was also more. More than he could see at that moment. Deep down, she couldn't put words to the fear that she'd never be able to give him enough. As a princess, her focus and her time would always be split between him and her people. As a woman, she could never carry the children he deserved. And no matter how much healing had happened here, between them and for each of them, that shamed her still. Hurt her deeply. And she would never bind them together in that hurt. She would never damage the love that they had for each other in that way. She thought of a thousand things she could say, all full of love, regret, sorrow and even some of joy. But instead she chose the words that had given her so much.

'Take what you need.'

The flash of fire in his eyes was all the notice she had before her world turned into one of pure sensual sensation. He rolled her in his arms so that she lay on the soft buttery leather of the sofa. His forearms were braced either side of her head, the flex of his powerful shoulders, so broad they made her feel crowded in the most delicious of ways. Completely surrounded by his body, but free to move as she wished, she arched into him, desperate for the touch of his skin.

His hands swept over her body, leaving trails of burning embers in their wake, heating her body, igniting an arousal that built touch by touch, kiss by kiss, until she was damp with need and panting with desire. His worship of her felt endless and she allowed herself to indulge purely in him and what he was giving them both.

He removed his jeans before gently pressing her thighs apart. They fell to his touch with shocking ease. She felt exposed but not vulnerable, on display but not for him: for *them*. She'd never felt such a sense of power, of confidence. Her heart beat just for him.

'Can you see what I see?'

She nodded, unable to look away from his face. She couldn't find the words to answer his question as his gaze covered every inch of her with exquisite intimacy. She wanted to reach for him, but she couldn't move. Wouldn't move. Everything she'd ever wanted was right there in that moment. And it was a moment that would have to last her a lifetime.

For a second she thought she saw him tremble as he came over her, but he covered her body with his, peppered her skin with kisses and touches and everything fell from her mind when she felt him at her entrance.

She felt the stillness come over him, demanding she look up at him. Demanding that she was with him in this exact moment.

'There will never be anyone else, do you understand that?'

She wanted to tell him the same. She wanted to tell him how much she loved him, but the words stuck in her throat a second too long and he seized that moment to slide into her with a thrust that felt endless and utterly complete.

Kjell's eyes drifted shut against his will as the feel of her encompassed him wholly. To be encased within her was a pleasure that was indescribable. Blood pounded in his veins, his heart lurched dramatically and the world as he knew it shifted for ever. He was marked by her. Branded.

And he wished to stay there for ever, his

body reacting to the tightening of hers, the way she gripped him, as if taking him even further into her, until he couldn't tell where he ended and she began.

Her back arched, bringing her chest upwards against his, and he snaked an arm behind her, holding her to him as he began to move, as the need in him became fierce and demanding, pushing them both towards an impossible conclusion. Sweat beaded the base of his spine as he thrust into her, her legs spreading for him, welcoming him deeper, her cries urging him on, hands pulling him harder against her, pleas demanding *more*, *faster*, *harder*.

Anything. He'd give her anything she wanted.

Sweat-slicked skin slid together, the heady erotic sounds driving their passion to maddening heights and depths. The cries of her pleasure a symphony he'd never tire of hearing, inflaming his need to wildness.

His orgasm pressed at the edges of his consciousness, but he thrust it back fiercely. He would fight to make this last, to make this something that Freya would never forget. Her head rolled back against the cushion as he drove into her. But he wanted to see her. To watch pleasure fill her gaze.

'Look at me,' he commanded selfishly as he encased himself to the hilt in her, relishing the gasp of pleasure that fell from lips above closed eyes. He withdrew so slowly it was a punishment for them both. 'Look at me,' he said, nearly leaving the warmth of her body completely. 'Please,' he begged, almost willingly losing his pride.

Her eyes burst open, a skyscape of clouds, stars and golden lights. The sight of it was the only thing that calmed the raging of his heart and loosened the leash needed on his restraint. He thrust into her, hard and fast, again and again, shamelessly driving them towards an orgasm so powerful that, when it broke, it shattered them both completely.

Kjell should have been in a sleep so deep that only Freya could reach him. But he wasn't. Sleep remained as elusive as the future. Soft, gentle sighs came from Freya's slumber and although he didn't want to leave her for even a minute of the time they had left, he knew what he had to do.

Slipping from beneath the fur throw that was warm from Freya's body, he pulled on his trousers and went to the stove, trying hard not to think too much about his actions. He put on a pot of coffee and turned to where he had last seen the AAR.

He retrieved the pages and placed them on

the table, barely able to look at them. He found a pen and flicked it between his fingers as he waited for the coffee to filter through. He hated that he was away from Freya. That he was wasting even a single second, but he needed to do this. Because he might not be able to do it after she left. He poured steaming, thick black coffee into his cup and, with determination steeling every single inch of his being, he sat down at the table and put pen to paper.

At sixteen hundred hours on the seventeenth of November...

The smell of coffee woke her. It wasn't the full hit of recently brewed coffee, more of a scent left in the air, long after consumption. Warm not hot, sweet not bitter. She felt the addictive heat of Kjell's body beside her and turned, taking in the look of serenity across features that were hardly ever so still. He seemed so much younger in that moment and she resisted the urge to trace the angles of his face for fear of waking him. One long arm was stretched out, his cheek resting on it, as if taking up as little of the deep sofa as possible. Even in sleep he was conscious of her and giving for her. Her heart curled in on itself as she realised that this was how she wanted to remember him.

Gently, she slid from the sofa and, wrapping herself in one of the throws, she went to the kitchen—pausing at the beautiful hand-made wooden table to see the AAR. Kjell's tight, neat handwriting filled page after page and she sighed, thankful that in this, at least, he had found his peace.

She pressed a finger against the cup half filled with coffee. It was cold. He must have worked through the last hours of darkness to complete the report. She cast a look back to where he slept, the sight filling her with a sense of warmth that took her by surprise.

She must have stayed like that for a while because it took her a moment to register the sound of the beep. Frowning, she had to hear it a few more times until she realised that it was her sat phone. She followed the next beep quickly, hoping to get to it before it woke Kjell. She took the phone with her into the boot room and risked the frigid icy cold as she opened the door and leaned out to get enough signal.

'Your Highness?'

'I'm here, Gunnar.'

'We will be with you in about thirty minutes.'

'I'll be ready,' she lied, her words frosting the cold air. The shiver that racked her body had nothing to do with the temperature and everything to do with the thought of leaving Kjell behind. She knew she should wake him, but she'd meant what she'd said the night before. She couldn't say goodbye. He might have given her the strength to embrace herself and face the public fallout, but no one could ask her to be strong enough to say goodbye to the man who had her heart.

Kjell heard the door to the cabin click shut and his heart lurched. Instantly he was awake, shock severing his connection to sleep. She was gone. He felt it more surely than he'd ever known anything before. Rage roared from his heart as he threw himself into last night's clothes. The sound of a helo nearby raced his pulse and rode him urgently forward. He had to see her, he had to stop her before she could leave.

He hadn't told her.

With an arm half in his jacket, his feet thrust into untied boots, he flung open the cabin door and hurled himself out into the snow. Clear blue skies taunted him and he could see Freya up ahead, getting into the helicopter.

His heart yelled her name and, as if she'd heard it, Freya turned at that exact moment and the hurt and sorrow in her gaze nearly felled him where he was. He stopped in his tracks, knowing that to go any further would only hurt them both.

But the damage was done. She'd left without saying goodbye. Without letting him tell her how much he loved her. His body was stuck, torn between the urge to pull her back to him and push her from him. She deserved to be the Princess she could be. To help others—as she always had. She could not do that and be with him. He knew that. He understood that duty and hated that it was a sacrifice they both would make over and over again.

There will never be anyone else.

His words from last night were whispered back to him on the wind as the helicopter lifted from the ground, the downwash throwing snow into the air, and he took them to the deepest parts of his soul.

CHAPTER ELEVEN

FREYA STARED AT the leafy green palace garden and instead saw snow. Cold tendrils snapped out at her and even in the spring sunshine of Svardia she couldn't get warm. Ever since she had left Dalarna two days ago, she had felt a fine shiver across her heart and it spread a chill through her body. This was what it felt like when a heart broke, she realised. She would have to take it deep within her, because she would live with it for the rest of her life.

Just then it was too raw to think of Kjell. To imagine what he was doing, what he was thinking, to wonder what he'd felt when he'd seen her disappear into the sky without having said goodbye.

Coward.

She cursed herself. He had deserved more than that and she hadn't been strong enough. She forced her hands to unfurl, not needing to look to know that her nails had imprinted crescents onto her palms. She should have told him. He should have heard the words.

But she *had* done the right thing by returning to Svardia. She could do so much good here and he could be so much more without her. A father. A good and loving husband.

There will never be anyone else.

His promise taunted the future she saw for him but she knew, *they* knew, it had been the right decision. Even if it left a scar on her heart that would never heal.

'Come.'

The command cut into her thoughts and Freya entered her brother's office, struck hard by the garish baroque design after the stunning simplicity of Kjell's cabin. She felt Aleksander's eyes assessing her. And suddenly that ice-cold thread winding around her heart turned to white-hot fury.

'How did it go?' Aleksander asked, his tone unusually gentle. But she wasn't ready to be gentled. No. She was ready to show a little of the less than perfect Princess she had learned that it was okay to be.

'You bastard.'

Anyone else would have flinched, but her brother simply stared back at her, waiting for an answer.

'You knew what you were doing when you

sent me there. You knew what had happened to Kjell.'

'Yes.'

'So, either you set me up to fail because you knew he would refuse the medal, or you set him up to face the most painful experience of his life and take the medal so that I would be free. Because you *knew* he would do that for me.'

'Yes.'

'That isn't an answer.' Her voice was harsh with accusation. She hated this cryptic, cold man her brother had become. Oh, she had absolutely no doubt that he'd be the perfect King, a good ruler for Svardia…but at what cost? 'When did you become so cruel?'

'When I realised just how much damage had been done to my little sisters by our parents' overzealous focus on monarchy.'

Freya reared back as if she'd been struck. They'd never really spoken of their parents' behaviour or treatment of them. It had been a sort of mute acceptance. Duty to the crown first and always. 'I don't…' She trailed off, unsure what to say.

'You are staying, yes? Maintaining your title and role?'

'Yes,' she said, a little unsure as to the swift turn of the conversation.

'And Bergqvist is refusing the medal?'

'Yes.'

There was a beat while her brother took this in. To the world, he might look as if he were deciding his next step, but Freya knew the speed with which his quick intelligence worked. Knew the way he considered people and decisions like pieces on a chessboard, weighing up all possible consequences of each move before it was made.

'Okay. The investiture is set for two weeks' time, but the Vårboll is on Friday. If you are staying, I shall expect you to be in attendance.'

Freya had forgotten about the Spring Ball held at the palace every year. She was nodding her agreement. 'I'm meeting with Stellan in—' she checked her watch '—about ten minutes. I still want to get the matter in front of parliament before the May recess.'

'Okay,' Aleksander replied. 'And you have a plan to address the press?'

And, just like that, Princess Freya of Svardia returned. Only this was a new Princess, and she couldn't help but see a little more assessment, a little more respect from her brother as they parried back and forth over the next seven minutes on the plan she had developed with Henna to reveal her infertility to the press. Aleksander insisted that they wait as long as possible before going public. But 'as long as possible' really only covered a few months. And the royal household's PR department would need to get going on it immediately.

And even in that short time Freya felt emotionally drained by the conversation. She would have to stretch these muscles, learn how to build up the emotional strength to become an advocate, not a victim. And Freya promised herself she would make the time to do so. She couldn't, wouldn't, go back to being half a princess—part fantasy image and only part herself. Svardia—and she—deserved nothing but her truth.

'When are you going to tell Marit?' Freya finally asked.

Aleksander looked up at her and Freya couldn't shake the feeling that there was something at play. Concern twisted in her heart for her sister. 'Aleksander. What have you done?'

'I'd rather wait just a little longer before informing her of your decision.' It didn't escape her notice that her brother had refused to answer her question.

'Sander,' she said, using his childhood name, calling on the long-ago bond between them.

'It's important.'

'Will you explain why?'

'Soon.'

A knock sounded on the office door.

'Yes?' Aleksander called.

Freya turned to see Henna in the doorway, looking apologetic for interrupting. 'I've put Stellan in your office,' she said to Freya.

Freya nodded and, looking to her brother, was surprised by the fierce look in the gaze Aleksander cast at Henna. Frowning, she turned back to Henna but she was already gone.

Freya opened her mouth to speak, but her brother spoke before she could even form the thought.

'Good luck with Stellan.'

'I'm going to need it,' she replied.

'Yes, you are,' she heard, as she left the King of Svardia's office.

Adrenaline flooded Kjell's body, his heart pounded so hard it should have given up long ago, sweat poured down across his skin. An hour-long punishing run and it still wasn't enough to rid him of the memory of watching Freya disappear into the sky in that helicopter.

He yanked open the door to the boot room, stripped himself naked and blindly made his way to the shower, refusing to even look at the sofa. It didn't work. He clenched his jaw against the cascade of erotic images that poured through his mind like the sigh that Freya made **just after she came. He was going to have to** burn that sofa unless he wanted to lose his god-damned mind.

He ignored the way the bathroom door slammed against the wall, ignored the shiver of disapproval he felt from his ancestors, ignored the instinctive reminder to feed the wood burner in case it went out.

He stepped into the shower, spun the dial to cold and braced himself against the tiles as the frigid spray poured down on his overheated skin. He was breathing hard and he couldn't honestly say that it was just down to the run. But arousal was so much better than the unappeased ache that he'd been left with the moment Freya had gone.

Her back arched in his mind, her head lost against the pillow, her breasts in his hands and her taste on his tongue, a long slow sweep of her clitoris and the cry of her pleasure in his ears. He took himself in hand, his grip like steel sliding slowly down to the hilt of his erection, and all he wanted was her hands. Her mouth. Her touch. The mockery of imitation sad and pathetic, enough to cut through his arousal.

He slammed the fleshy side of a fist against the wall. Once. Then twice. It wasn't right. Something deep inside was itching and scratching as if to get out and he hated it.

To face it you need to change the way you

think about it. To not see it as a threat, but as an experience.

His own words came back to haunt him. He flicked off the shower and grabbed a towel, drying himself with ruthless strokes that grazed his skin. He pulled fresh clean clothes on and poured a cup of coffee, turning to lean back against the sideboard.

He looked over to find the note Freya had left him.

You should go home now, Kjell.

His gut clenched. He saw his father—the disappointment that would be waiting for him. He'd failed again. As a soldier. As a son. He clenched his jaw. But he wouldn't fail as a friend. Before he could change his mind, he picked up his phone and keyed in a number he knew by heart. The international dialling tone sounded harsh, impatient, and for a second he thought the call would ring out.

'*Sì?*' Distracted—irritated, even—the tone wasn't what he'd expected. '*Pronto?*'

'Marella?'

'*Cristo*, Kjell? Is that you?' Enzo's wife asked in English.

'Yes.'

Static shifted in his ear as if she had covered

the speaker. Faint Italian words sounded in the background and the static shifted again, making way for a deep sigh.

'Are you okay?' she asked him.

He barked out a sad laugh. 'That was my question to ask you,' he chided. He could imagine her smiling a little, but he knew she was waiting for him to answer. 'Yes. No. Maybe?'

'That would be my answer to the question you wanted to ask,' she said quietly.

There was a moment of silent grief shared across skies and countries.

'I'm sorry I didn't—'

'No. No, there's no apologies here,' she interrupted him before he could even finish. 'None, Kjell. Enzo was a soldier. It was more than a uniform, for him as much as you. I knew that before I married him and I knew it when I... when I buried him. He was and always will be the love of my life. And I wouldn't have changed him for the world.' The strength of her words, the fierceness of her love—he felt it in his heart.

'He saved them, Marella. The children he protected. He saved every single one of them.' He couldn't give her much, but he could give her that. He heard the tears that Enzo's wife cried in that moment, felt them as if they were his own.

'*Grazie*, Kjell. Thank you.'

'I should go—'

'Wait,' she said, cutting off his attempt to end the call. 'He would have wanted...' Her breath hitched and she tried again. 'He would have wanted you to take the medal.'

'What?' He felt the blood drain from his face.

'The guys were talking about it at the wake. The medal you were refusing. Enzo wouldn't have wanted that, Kjell,' she said, the rebuke in her tone gentle but clear. 'He always said that you deserved more than one for what you'd done over the years.'

Tears thickened her voice as she thanked him for calling and he felt his own rise up, not feeling an ounce of shame for the evidence of his own grief. They spoke for a few more minutes, made promises to visit each other as soon as possible, and Kjell ended the call feeling bruised but not beaten.

Once again, his gaze drifted to the crumpled note Freya had left him.

You should go home now, Kjell.

Freya had left him without saying goodbye. Without hearing the words she deserved to hear. Screwing up the note she'd left him, he threw it on the flames of the wood burner.

Kjell was done with unfinished business.

* * *

Freya took one last look at the selfie her sister had just sent her. Marit was pressed up next to a man handsome in all the ways that Kjell was not: dark, lean, silver-eyed, with just enough of a glint of danger to match her wayward younger sister. But it was the smile on Marit's face that had caught Freya's notice. The purity of it, the unconscious joy of it, warmed the ache in Freya's heart. She wasn't sure what games her brother had been playing, but for her sister it had turned out happily at least. There would be time to catch up with all the dramatic events, but now was not it. All Freya needed to know was that her beloved sister had found a man who loved her as she deserved to be loved.

Putting down the phone, Freya looked at herself in her bedroom mirror, turning from to one side to the other. Hundreds of thousands of crystals sewn into champagne-coloured silk sparkled in the light, sending a shimmer rippling across the exquisite art deco pattern made with the hand-sewn beads. Thin straps caressed her shoulders, connecting to a deep V neck that stopped a little below demure and just above risqué. The corset that hugged her torso stopped at a belt around the waist before dropping into layers of tulle mixed with silk, making the beads look like rivulets of water falling to the floor and into a train that trailed behind her.

With her hair plaited and pinned back into a neat nest above her neck, she looked exactly like the royal she was. Henna had left the Prussian blue velvet box her brother had sent her on the dressing table. Freya knew what it was. She had worn it at the Officers' Ball in Vienna, which had counted—for the most part—as her coming out or debutante ball.

Wearing the tiara now, Freya felt as if she was reaffirming her promise to her family, her country even: the promise of her duty. And that her brother had thought of it made her heart soften towards him, hoping that the boy she'd once known was still in there somewhere. She lifted the lid on the box containing the family heirloom, knowing the diamond-encrusted gold tiara matched her dress perfectly.

This was her brother's first Vårboll and it would be nothing short of exquisite. Champagne had been brought in from the choicest vintners, caviar from sustainably sourced fisheries, and the music was being performed by the finest of Svardia's musicians.

International royalty, global dignitaries, billionaires, tech magnates and titans of industry.

They had all been invited to help Aleksander bring Svardia into the twenty-first century as a powerful player on the world's stage. And until he found a wife, Freya would be there to help him.

She cast a last look at herself in the mirror, her pale gaze haunted by the memory of snow and heat and the man who had her heart, before turning away. Flexing her hands in the hope of shaking off some of the cold that nipped at her fingers, Freya caught the unrestrained sorrow in Henna's gaze.

'Henna,' Freya gently admonished. 'Please don't. It's fine. *I'm* fine. Really.'

Henna gave her one long considering look and nodded reluctantly. Freya had told her only the bare bones of what had happened in Dalarna, half afraid that if she spoke any more the words would open the fissure in her heart and she would break completely.

'Let's go,' Freya said, marshalling her courage to become the Princess she wanted to be. She would never be perfect. She had learned that, not because Kjell had made her feel anything less, but precisely because he'd made her feel perfect in her imperfections. Now, Freya wanted to be *herself.* Only by accepting that would she be able to survive the fallout of her infertility. For her family to survive it.

* * *

They approached the staircase that led down
into the Rilderdal Palace ballroom from the
first-floor balcony that wrapped around the
grand chamber, and Freya paused for a moment to take in the majesty of the sight.

Chandeliers of glass cut a thousand times
over a hundred years ago hung from the domed
ceiling high above them, scattering light onto
the gold filagree and inlay on the mouldings
and cornices and shining down on the floor
below. Waiters in red fine wool jackets served
flutes of champagne and canapés on silver
trays, candelabras provided atmosphere beside exquisite flower displays trailing ivy and
eucalyptus from fountains of white peonies.

Opulence. It was the only word that came to
mind. Her gaze grazed emeralds in earlobes,
diamonds on fingers, rubies on wrists and sap-
phires nestled in bosoms of the female guests.
Gold, silver and just as many jewels graced the
cufflinks of the men, enough to fill the greatest of war chests.

A war chest the like of which she could hope-
fully one day put to use for causes that affected
not just Svardian people but *all* people. Determination schooled features that she would once
have hidden behind a picture-perfect mask. She
would hide herself no more.

'Freya—'

'It's time for me to make my *grand* entrance,' Freya interrupted, her tone strong, and feeling it too. She had faced freezing cold water, she had faced the loss of every single thing she had ever wanted, and she was still here.

She arrived at the top of the staircase and the music faded into the background. Slowly descending into the Spring Ball, she used the confidence Kjell had helped her to find in her own strength to be the Princess that Svardia deserved—that *she* deserved.

Her brother waited for her at the bottom of the staircase with his arm out to hers in welcome. Despite their tense exchange earlier in the week, they'd quickly and easily forgiven each other and focused their attempts to ensure Svardia thrived under Aleksander's rule.

As she was introduced and reintroduced to the most important of people, she found a rhythm that was familiar but also new. It held traces of who she had once been, but also who she would become. And while it didn't chase away the cold that nipped at her heart, it did appease it a little.

She was just about to greet the Minister for Agriculture when she felt her brother's arm tense beneath her hand. Looking up and finding his gaze locked over her shoulder, she turned to find the source of his agitation...and her heart stopped.

Making his way towards her in the full dress uniform of the Svardian Armén, clean-shaven, tall, powerful and determined, Kjell looked utterly magnificent. Not only did he not look out of place—he outshone every man there. Her starved gaze took him in, the crisp cream coat with gold brocade and Prussian blue sash would have been eye-catching on anyone, but Kjell wore it to devastating effect. The display of medals across his chest made her hand clench in memory of the honour he and his friend deserved. The dark trousers in fine wool showed off the powerful muscles of his thighs, their forward march towards her seemingly unending and impossible to stop.

Female heads turned in his wake, lascivious gazes on every face. Men watched with eyes full of jealousy, envy, some just as lustful. But every single person parted for him without question or direction, they simply moved for him.

Freya's heart leapt painfully in her chest, and for the first time since leaving Dalarna her body was warmed by a flush that crested over her like a wave. For the space of a single breath her heart soared, believing that he had come to claim her so that they could be together finally.

But then her brother shifted beside her and she remembered. Remembered that it couldn't be. That, without a title, he would never be allowed to marry her. And on an exhalation a heartache so acute filled her lungs she feared she would never recover.

Intense arctic blue eyes held hers with a thousand promises and apologies, as if he'd known that this would hurt her but that he'd not been able to stay away. Her hand dropped from Aleksander's arm and she took one step towards Kjell, then another, even though everything in her wanted to *run* to him.

They met in the middle of the ballroom floor, bound in silence by a spell only love could weave. He bowed to her, low and deep. Ignoring the barely hushed, curious whispers of the guests around them, Freya curtsied to him so deeply that there was no doubt to anyone watching that she saw him as her equal. No matter what rank or title he did or did not have, she would always meet him as such.

Kjell straightened to see Freya curtsy deep into the silk of her skirts. Her head bent in deference to him was a sight so humbling he felt red slashes form across his cheeks. The gentle slope of her breast encased by the jewelled corset offered him the most vulnerable part of her—and he felt as if she had known it, had offered it to him on purpose; the soldier in him roared against the fragility of her heart, but the man in him growled contentedly in appeasement.

He held his hand out to hers and when she placed her palm against his, his heart ached to realise that this was the *true* home he'd been exiled from. Eight years he'd been without her and there would be so many more years to come. But this, *this* he was selfish enough to take.

The tap of the conductor's baton called the musicians to attention and Kjell brought Freya into a hold, his palm pressing against her back, the heat of her body calming him like nothing else had ever done in all the years since he'd first met her.

Freya looked up at him, her amber eyes trusting and utterly uncaring of the surroundings. With one hand in his, she bent to pick up the skirt of her dress with the other, and his heart pounded just to see how incredible she looked, the beads on her dress not even close to the sparkling beauty of her eyes.

The music started the moment he took them into the first step of a waltz and the rest of the world disappeared. She was alive in his hands, her movements lithe and graceful, her natural poise so profoundly balancing to his erratic heart, he feared he genuinely might not survive without her. But it was her trust in him that moved him the most. Her trust so complete that he could lead her anywhere and she would follow. Her trust that even then he would never lead her away from the duty they had both sacrificed so much for. A sacrifice he would continue to make. But only if he was finally able to speak the words in his heart.

'You left without saying goodbye.' His voice was low, audible only to her.

Her eyes flared, but still she didn't look away. 'I... I couldn't. I couldn't say it,' she confessed, pain breaking through the words. 'I'm sorry.'

'Don't be.' He looked away only briefly, catching Freya's brother's glare. 'I wouldn't have been able to let you go,' he admitted, the truth of his statement evident in the raw edge of his voice.

'But you can now?' she asked. He pulled her just a little closer into his hold, his legs sweeping through the layers of tulle and silk and beading, desperate to feel the warmth of her body.

'You were born for this, Freya, not *into* it. The title, the role...these things were meant for you.'

I was meant for you, a part of him cried, but he thrust it aside. For her.

'But you need to know—'

Her hand tightened in his hold, stalling his words, as if half wanting to stop him and half wanting him to never stop. He blew out a breath, steeling himself against the inevitable pain that would follow his words. But he stood by them. And she deserved more than anything to hear them.

'I love you.' His voice was a whisper but the power of those words struck like a bell's toll that changed their worlds. Her eyes filled, but not a single tear fell. Amber shimmering into gold. 'I will always stand by your decision to remain royal. But I will always love you.'

Her lips trembled until she speared her bottom lip with her teeth and he wished for all the world to reach for it, set it free with the pad of his thumb, but he felt every single set of eyes in the entire room on his back, watching intently, trying to fathom what was happening.

'Eight years ago, we didn't get the chance to do things properly. And when you left Dalarna...' His heart shattered all over again at the memory of her getting in the helicopter and disappearing into the snow-filled sky. 'We need to say goodbye.'

For the first time since he'd appeared, Freya

dropped her gaze from his face and whispered, 'What if I can't?'

The waltz was reaching a crescendo, she could hear it and feel it in her breast.

'You can. Because you're the strongest person I know.'

Breath shuddered in Freya's chest and everything hurt. Her body, her skin, her heart… But instead of feeling the icy frigid grasp that had held her heart since leaving Kjell in Dalarna, a pulse of warmth beat within her. His words, his love, igniting a single ember into an inferno that bloomed and twirled and twisted until she felt the truth of it feed her, forge her strength anew. She looked up to find his head angled over her shoulder, the stark line of his jaw, the powerful and proud man she loved whole-heartedly. A man she would never touch again after that night.

She felt a single tear escape down her cheek. 'I love you,' she whispered, even though it broke her. It hurt and wrecked her, but he deserved to hear it too. 'I will never stop loving you.'

His jaw clenched, the muscle flaring, and when he turned his gaze to her, the raw pain in his eyes was only matched by her own. The music came to a crashing climactic conclusion and he drew them to a stop in the centre of the ballroom, watched by a hundred pairs of eyes.

He released her from his hold, stepped back, bowed low and deep, and this time the perfect Princess forgot all about etiquette, forgot to curtsy at all. Struck completely still, Freya watched as Kjell turned on his heel and left the ballroom.

On the far side of the ballroom Aleksander watched Bergqvist walk away from his sister, his jaw clenched and fury pounding in his veins. He was about to go to Freya when Henna appeared by his side. His sister's lady-in-waiting looked as angry as he felt.

'Fix it,' she commanded. Two little words in a tone that no one ever dared speak to him in.

He raised an imperious eyebrow that had quelled heads of state and countless politicians.

'I don't care what you have to do, just fix it.'

And she stalked off, leaving him just as confused as he always was whenever she was around. He looked up to see Kjell disappear through the large doors of the palace ballroom and decided that the time for subtlety was over.

CHAPTER TWELVE

KJELL LEFT THE palace in a daze that no self-respecting soldier would tolerate. His heart pounded in his ears and his eyes were full of the last look Freya had given him, leaving him half blind and deaf and utterly vulnerable to attack.

It had been the right thing, but it had left him devastated in a way he would never recover from. Even Enzo's voice in his mind was quiet. Kjell made his way down cobbled streets in the old part of Torfarn, gently illuminated by streetlights wrapped in wrought iron filigree. He stumbled, feeling drunk without having touched a drop of alcohol and cursed, desperate to get himself under control before he arrived at his destination. Everything in him made him want to leave, to return to Sweden. But Freya had been right. He had to go home. Even if he wasn't sure that Svardia was it, he needed to see his parents. Needed to face his father.

His mother and father had moved out of the palace a few years ago as Brynjar had needed space for a workshop, which had been impossible in the palace staff housing. Kjell wondered if his mother missed it, having spent her life surrounded by the hundreds of live-in staff, the constant buzz he remembered from his childhood that had made integration into the army seamless.

After three hours of walking, he came to the front door of a modest house on a quiet suburban street. At two in the morning, he was surprised to find a gentle light glowing from the back of the house where his father's workshop was. He made his way through to the garden with the silent steps instinctive to a soldier, but still his father was waiting for him. The wide wooden door of the garage was open, revealing the workbench where Brynjar Bergqvist sat, polishing a small piece of metal.

His father peered at him over wire-framed glasses and, although he didn't smile or seem surprised, Kjell was half convinced he heard love in his father's voice when he said, 'Welcome home.'

Kjell nodded, unable to speak past the lump in his throat. He wished he could be stronger, wished he didn't have this need crawling beneath his skin, desperately reaching for something he could never have. But he knew that he needed to face this.

'It's good to be back,' Kjell replied.

'Is it?' his father asked, seeing more than he would ever say.

'No. Not really,' Kjell said, not having the will to mask the hurt with a laugh.

His father kicked out a stool for Kjell to sit on as he carried on tinkering with the piece of equipment half dismantled on the bench. Kjell sat on the stool and leaned back against the side of the workshop, letting the sounds of the night seep deep into his soul.

'Start at the beginning,' his father commanded, as if knowing that he needed to talk but wasn't quite sure how to.

With a voice rusty and raw, Kjell told his father about his first deployment with Enzo, what it had been like working with the UN. Kjell admitted how hard it had been coming back to Svardia, knowing that he couldn't stay but also feeling guilt for not wanting to stay.

Brynjar poured a couple of inches of the *akvavit* he kept in the drawer of his old workbench and passed a glass to Kjell. They drank their first mouthful to the woman they both loved, the second to absent friends and the third to the old Norse god of war, Odin, for allowing Kjell to return alive. The alcohol burned

Kjell's throat and stung his eyes like a young boy taking his first sip. But his father never said a word.

'I'm not sure I can be a solider any more,' Kjell admitted, the words scraping his throat raw and unable to meet his father's eye. He held his breath until his father's next words, surprised by the question.

'Why did you want to be a soldier?'

Because of you.

But they didn't have the kind of relationship that would welcome such raw honesty in that deep visceral way.

'Because I wanted to serve my country. Because I wanted to give myself to a greater cause. But... I'm not sure it's enough any more.'

'Do you know why I left the *Försvarsmakten*?'

'Because Mum needed to be here?'

When there wasn't a reply, Kjell looked up at his father, realising for the first time that they'd never actually spoken of it. He had always assumed that his father had sacrificed his career for his wife and that resentment had been thrust so deep that it had kept Brynjar Bergqvist short worded and silent. He realised in that moment that he'd done his father a great disservice in thinking so.

Brynjar nodded sadly into the silence, as if

divining his son's thoughts. He grabbed a stool and brought it beside Kjell and sat, finally putting aside the piece of metal that had consumed his attention.

His father took a deep breath. 'No. I left because I found that my heart had a new duty. A new purpose that would always come before King and country. And I didn't feel that I could honestly give Sweden my whole allegiance when it would always be elsewhere.'

'Mum was that purpose,' Kjell said, beginning to see his father in a different light.

'Yes,' his father admitted. 'And you.'

Kjell felt the sting of wetness press against his eyes. 'I'm not sure I'm worthy of it.'

'The fact that you even doubt that makes it clear that *I* am the one not worthy.'

Shock marred Kjell's features and heart.

Brynjar frowned into the distance. 'Your mother, she is the one who is good with words. I find them…difficult. My father? Now, he was truly terrible. At least you are better than I. It will bode well for your children.'

His heart lurched. 'I'm not sure that…' He bit off the words that cut his heart in two. There would and could never be anyone other than Freya. But even if they had come together, her infertility meant that was an impossibility. But something in his heart turned over. The memory of the children Enzo had saved, the savage destruction of communities he'd witnessed, the thousands of orphans he'd encountered over the years. There were so many children who needed and deserved the kind of unconditional love Freya was capable of. That *he* was capable of. The thought vanquished what he'd been about to tell his father and planted a seed in his heart that would one day grow into something more beautiful than he could ever have imagined.

'I think you have found a new duty,' his father said, nodding sagely. 'Well, she is definitely worthy of it.'

Kjell looked over at his father in shock, and not only because of the wry humour in his father's tone. 'You know?'

'About Freya? Yes,' Brynjar concluded.

'How?' Surely he hadn't caused that much of a scene at the palace.

'Because I told him.' The strong, authoritarian voice came from the other side of the garden and Kjell's head snapped up to see the King of Svardia. Pinpricks of shock and self-recrimination covered his skin. No one should have been able to sneak up on him like that. But he was beginning to suspect that Aleksander wasn't quite what everyone seemed to think he was.

In his peripheral vision Kjell saw his father

pick up the piece of machinery and resume his focus on the object as if the King of Svardia wasn't there in his garden at three o'clock in the morning.

As Aleksander approached, his lazy gait might have fooled many but, now that Kjell was aware, he saw right through Freya's brother's assumed ease. Tension thrummed on the air as Kjell stood to meet his King, the informality of the setting making any display of courtesy awkward. Not to mention anger at what Aleksander had put Freya through by sending her to him in Dalarna.

'You sent her to me in the middle of a storm,' he growled, uncaring of hierarchy or power. The man in front of him had put the woman he loved in jeopardy.

'She was never in any danger,' dismissed the King of Svardia.

'Threat isn't always physical,' he replied, knowing how significant the emotional damage could have been.

'Which is why I sent her to you.'

Kjell scoffed, and purposely gave the man his back in a display of such disrespect even his usually stoic father frowned.

'Frankly, Kjell, I couldn't care less if you spend the rest of your life with your back to me. But is that what you would do to my sister?'

'I have given her the only thing I can,' he said

bitterly. 'Her freedom. If I kept her she would never be fulfilled. She would never reach the potential she has within her. She would never do all that she could do for Svardia.'

'But you would if you could? Keep her? Love her?' The soft word sounded awkward and unusual in the harsh tone Aleksander had used, but that barely scraped Kjell's notice.

'With every single ounce of my being. Unquestionably and unendingly,' he said, the truth of his words shining bright, and he felt the unfurling of an impossible hope fill his breast.

'It will require the sacrifice of everything you know. Your freedom, your independence. Your allegiance would be to her and your privacy would never be your own again.' This time there was an undertone that Kjell couldn't ignore. It spoke quietly but deeply of secrets and hurt, and all but demanded to be heard, listened to and seriously considered. Kjell did Aleksander the courtesy of doing so. But when he met his King's gaze and spoke, his voice was level, powerful and sure.

'She has my heart. Everything else is immaterial.'

Aleksander nodded once. 'Good. Then let's get to work.'

Freya's cheeks hurt, her heart ached, her stomach twisted, but she smiled as the group of people around her all cheered. She accepted the congratulations of her team, Stellan's teary-eyed thanks and the begrudging acceptance of the minister she'd persuaded to help bring Stellan's worthy fight to parliament. Freya might have strong-armed him into it, but she knew that the minister wouldn't have agreed if he hadn't believed in the cause himself, or thought that there was hope of getting it through.

This was why she had returned. Why she had made the choice she had. And if she was given that same choice again, she'd make the same decision, even knowing how much it hurt to leave Kjell behind. To leave her heart behind.

With him she could achieve small steps, but here she could make giant leaps. And the same could be said of Kjell. With her, he would only take small steps towards the life he deserved. And he deserved so much more.

Henna stood at her shoulder with a smile so beautiful it eased some of Freya's hurt. 'I knew you could do it.'

'Of course I could.' Freya shrugged. 'It only took us four years,' she replied, thinking of how much she had invested in Stellan's cause, of the sacrifices the people in this room had also made.

'Do you know what you will turn your attention to next?' Henna asked, her gaze careful but watching.

Freya started nodding before she answered. 'Yes,' she replied, feeling the solemnity of it rise within her to fill spaces that would never be filled by a child. 'Yes, I do.'

Kjell had been right. Lending an empathetic ear, giving an understanding voice to women who might not have the ability to speak for themselves had become an all-consuming need. Freya felt it; all around the world people were experiencing this incredible moment where, instead of being scared and fearful, they had the opportunity to question, consider, explore what it meant to be who they were. To be *curious* about how they identified, who they wanted to be with. To be flexible rather than rigid in their feelings about it. The question of what it was to be female, feminine, womanly, *woman* was so bound up in the body and what it could do, that when it couldn't or *wouldn't* do what it was supposed to do it rocked the deepest foundations of identity. And without support or understanding that could be a devastatingly terrifying place to be. She never wanted anyone to feel that way and if she could bring even the slightest attention or support to ease people into that place of curiosity rather than fear then… *then* she would find peace.

She would never have her own children. She knew that. Surrogacy was a possibility, but emotionally Freya knew that wasn't for her. But on the other side of infertility, she thought of all the children who needed homes and families and all the love that she was capable of feeling. She knew that, just as surrogacy wasn't an option for her, adoption wouldn't be an option for others. But she marvelled at this wonderful world where those choices were even possible. Understanding might just have to catch up a little. It wouldn't be for everyone, but that was okay. At least it was there for some.

In the blink of an eye, she imagined herself with two little children and wondered at the audacity of the once perfect Princess daring to be a single mother to two adopted children.

It would be perfect, she heard Kjell whisper in her mind and this time it warmed her rather than hurt.

'I hate to draw you away, but the Investiture is due to begin in ninety minutes, and you might want to change.'

Freya's heart thumped at the reminder. She knew that she'd been pushing the event that would have seen Kjell awarded the medal of Valour to the back of her mind, had perhaps even been hoping to miss it. But Henna seemed unusually determined to ensure that she was not only ready but also presentable.

She looked down at her clothes. 'What is wrong with what I'm wearing?'

Eighty-seven minutes later, a prettily dressed Freya was half laughing as Henna pushed her up to the side entrance on the lower level of the ballroom. The space had been transformed for the Investiture with a red velvet stage fitting the baroque style, and the ballroom was half full of guests. Unlike the other night, there was an excited hum. Freya had always preferred investitures to balls, where the people of Svardia came to be honoured for both everyday heroism and extraordinary acts of valour equally.

She caught her brother's gaze from the far end of the stage, standing in the frame of the side entrance opposite. For a moment his eyes were warm, smiling—and they shared a moment of real joy at being part of the royal family—before the shutters came down and the boy she remembered from their youth disappeared behind the mask of the man he had become. She felt the loss but had long given up hope of trying to reach deep enough to know what had happened to the smiling, laughing teenager she barely remembered.

The gentle music in the background changed

and increased in volume and the commencement music played as brother and sister came onto the stage to meet in the middle.

The genuine joy at the attendees' pride and awe in the day soothed some of the hurt that had taken up residence in Freya's heart. And she was watching a little girl reach up for her daddy to take her in his arms when she heard a name that cut through her thoughts immediately.

She forced her attention onto the crowd of smiling faces until a figure approached the stage so familiar, so handsome, so heartbreaking that she had to blink several times just to refocus. She fisted her hands to hide the fine tremors tumbling through her body and clasped them together, hoping that no one had seen.

Her heart thudded and she wasn't sure she dared risk a glance at him, but couldn't hold out against the desperate need to see him. To take him in. Her eyes flickered between him and the audience and she realised that Kjell's incredible focus was on her brother and only him. It hurt just a little until she realised it gave her the opportunity to stare as long and openly as she wanted to.

Unlike the last time she had seen him in the ballroom, Kjell was dressed in the mess dress uniform, the deep blue-black wool of the rolled

collar jacket and waistcoat contrasted with the
ivory white shirt, reminding her of the view of
the snow-covered forest from the windows of
the cabin. Somehow the more civilian style of
suit made him look less civilised. She could
feel the raw power of him vibrating beneath
his skin. It called to something deep within
her, something that raged at being ignored or
denied as Kjell continued to focus solely on
her brother.

He was taking the medal.

A part of her wanted to stop the ceremony,
feared that he was only doing this for her, not
because he'd finally made peace with the trau-
matic events that had caused the death of his
closest friend. But when Kjell finally stood before her brother, rather than bowing his head
to receive the award, he did something else
entirely.

Her brother swept his arm in invitation and
Kjell lowered to his knees. Confusion twisted
through Freya like a tornado. Medals were
awarded at a bow, not a kneel. Only…only titles were bestowed at a kneel.

Goosebumps rose over her skin, her arms,
her neck, her breasts. She stared at her brother,
his back now to her as he reached for the cere-
monial sword, and Freya felt tears press against
her eyes before her mind caught up fully with

what was happening in front of her. The consort for the first two legitimate heirs to the throne had to have a title; it was a lesson she'd learned over and over and over again.

Could this be really happening?

On the opposite side of the stage, hidden in the shadows just beyond her brother's shoulder, she caught a glimpse of Henna, her eyes bright, shining and a smile so beautiful, so encouraging. Her oldest friend, her lady-in-waiting, nodded as if divining her thoughts from across the room.

Freya's heart beat so loudly in her ears she couldn't hear the words said by her brother, but she knew them in her heart as her brother took the sword that had been in their family for five generations and, in reward for his honour, loyalty and valour, touched the sword to one shoulder then the next.

In that moment Freya realised what he'd done. What he'd sacrificed. Kjell would never be a soldier, he would never return to duty. After all she'd tried to do, all she'd tried to protect him from...

'Rise, Viscount Fjalir,' her brother said.

Freya was torn, agony roaring through her at his sacrifice, but that selfish need burning in her chest wanted to run to him. And then, as Kjell stood, his eyes turned to her and, as if reading her fear, her fury, he stalked towards her—absolutely nothing civilised in his gaze.

Uncaring of her surroundings and utterly in thrall to this man, she took a step backwards and another as he kept advancing—the sheer force of his determination pushing her and crowding her into the shadows of the curtained section of the stage. Distantly she was aware of the music resuming and the low hum of the crowd as her brother led the participants off to the reception further into the interior of the palace. But her mind was only on the terrible sacrifice Kjell had just made.

'What have you done?' she asked him in a trembling voice as she stared up at the man she wanted to pull to her as much as push away. Arctic eyes flared at the sound of her voice, his legs only finally coming to a halt as her back pressed up against the wall. The breadth of his shoulders surrounded her, protected her, warmed her. She leaned towards him against her will, desperate to feel the heat of him. 'You stopped being a soldier?' she asked, the quiver in her voice betraying the emotion she felt for him.

'Yes.' His response was swift and sure.

'Kjell—' She tried to take control of the situation, but he wouldn't let her.

'Congratulations on getting Stellan to par-

liament,' he whispered as he raised a hand to cup her cheek with the gentlest of touches, as if he wasn't completely sure that she was real.

She'd been about to turn away from his touch in shame, but surprise stole through her instead. 'How did you...?' Ignoring her question, Kjell's eyes searched the depths of hers, as if hoping to divine a truth she'd desperately tried to keep a secret.

'I think you've been trying to protect me,' he said, his tone solemn, stalling any attempt to hide from the man she loved with all of her being. She bit her lip, not in the least surprised that he knew her well enough to realise exactly what she'd been doing. 'I think,' he said, 'that you pushed me away because you think I deserve something you believe you're not capable of giving me.'

Freya tried to hold his gaze as he stared down at her, a stare that displayed the magnitude of hurt she had left him with.

'I think you've done this because you felt you didn't have a choice. But now you do.'

'Kjell...' Her heart broke for him, but he shook his head, his eyes not leaving hers.

'I couldn't have stayed a soldier. I didn't believe in it any more. It wasn't who I wanted to be any more.' He leaned back a little, giving her enough space to take his next words seriously.

'My duty, my allegiance? All yours. My heart? You've had it since I was twenty. My hand you can have now and for ever.'

He could see the emotions warring in her eyes, the guilt traversing across them. 'I know that you thought my exile prevented me from coming home. But all it did was make me realise that my home isn't a place, it's not Svardia or even my parents. It is—and has been ever since the moment I first laid eyes on you— with you.'

'But, Kjell...' she said, her heart breaking for the children she would never be able to give him. He cupped her jaw, his thumb sweeping away a tear she hadn't realised had fallen. She trembled in his arms, the force of emotion hitting her like a train. 'I love you so much,' she said. 'I love you so much that I want to say yes, I want to keep you with me for ever. You make me all the things that are truly me and more. I have laughed with you, cried with you, learned with you... You complete me,' she said simply and truthfully. But you deserve more, and I would hate to tie you to what we will never have.'

Kjell felt the agony in her heart, knew how much it cost her to even say it. 'My only thought is to all we *can* have,' he said, pressing kisses across her cheeks, her nose, her forehead. 'We will adopt a hundred children if you want, or instead we will be happy pouring all our love into each other and the people of Svardia. The future is nothing to fear, Freya, it is to be shared and relished. It was my job to protect you. And, facing the future ahead of us, I will continue to do that with my heart, my body and my life.'

She looked up at him with those hypnotic whisky-coloured eyes—wide and, yes, full of trust—and nodded, shifting the foundations beneath the wall of anxiety around his heart. Fear by fear, block by block, those walls began to tumble, until nothing was left but a love so sure, so strong and pure that it would never dim—no matter the years that came and went. It would never tarnish, no matter the struggles that were overcome, and would never be less for anything that was taken from them. Their love was abundant, in that moment and all the moments to come.

'Princess Freya of Svardia,' he said, pressing his forehead to hers, covering her body with his, 'will you marry me?'

Freya's heart pounded in her chest, joy a sparkle that started at the floor and rose up to surround them both in light and love and hope for the future.

'Viscount Fjalir, it would be my honour.'

And then, as if he refused to miss a single second now that he knew they could be together for ever, he pulled her into a kiss that promised so much joy and so much wickedness her heart didn't know whether to roar with need or love and Freya finally settled on feeling them both at the same time, as befitting the way her solider, her love, her protector made her feel, then, now and always.

EPILOGUE

Five years later...

THE SOUND OF children's laughter danced on the warm summer breeze flowing into the cabin through the open windows. Freya was talking on the phone, finalising the details of a meeting following her return to Svardia at the end of the month. And while her mind quickly provided the necessary information, her heart was calling her down to the lake, to where her husband was teaching their three children to swim.

'Your Highness?'

'Just make sure that the delegate's husband is invited on the tour too.'

'Yes, ma'am.'

'Are we done?' Freya asked, unable to keep the childlike impatience from her tone. A gentle laugh and an assurance that they were indeed done was enough to have Freya hanging up and grabbing the sunscreen she had come to find when the phone had rung. As she followed the steps down from the deck wrapping around their cabin and through the well-trodden path of trampled grass bisecting the large wildflower meadow towards the lake, Freya paused.

She could just make out the sounds of Kjell's voice, the tone he used for their children so full of love that she almost couldn't contain her reaction to it. She could just about see their eldest, Alarik, who they had adopted at the age of six, standing knee deep in the water, all skinny limbs and sharp angles. His thick dark hair, soaked from the lake, swept back from his forehead as he laughed when Kjell was attacked by the much smaller, blonder forms of Mikael from one side and Malin from the other.

Freya inhaled slow and deep, relishing this moment. Years ago, she had promised herself that she would take the time to process her emotions, the reality of her diagnosis and her feelings about it and herself. And—she nodded to herself—she had done. It had become part habit now that when she felt the need sweep over her she would take that pause and recognise all the good that had come into her life with a sense of welcome that was joyous.

So much had happened since her first visit

to Dalarna and she wouldn't change a single thing. All the assessments and meetings needed to ensure that the adoption process for Alarik first, and then later Malin and Mikael, who had come together as siblings, was successful had been worth it. At first Freya had feared that, given her position, the public nature of her life and role and what that would mean for her children, it might have been an outright 'no' from the agency they had approached. But the amazing team of people there had given Freya, Kjell and their children all the help and support they'd needed in the transition into a family.

In the early years, a lot of effort had been put into working with the press rather than against them and without it Freya genuinely believed it would have been a much harder road. But it had been Marit's suggestion to see them as collaborators rather than adversaries. And now the Svardian press, and increasingly the international press, were ferociously protective of their children and what was written about them.

Freya smiled in anticipation of Marit's arrival in a few hours with her husband and their children and felt her heart expand with happiness. The love she had for her sister had developed in the last few years from one that bordered on maternal to one that was now balanced and firmly based in sisterhood. It felt right and good, and Freya knew without a doubt much of that was due to Marit's husband, who had given her sister the space and love she needed to be confident in who she was and it was one of the things that Freya was eternally grateful for.

Excitement swirled in her chest as she thought of Aleksander and his family, also joining them the following day. With their parents in Svardia, prepared to handle any royal duties, the siblings would soon all be together. Although it had been difficult for their parents to adapt to the changes that Aleksander had made during his rule, they had come to see the benefits of his decisions. And although it was highly unlikely that the love between their parents and her and her siblings would ever be relaxed and free, it was beginning to get easier.

'Daddy!' screamed Malin as he picked her up, cradled her in his arms and dropped down into the water, splashing Mikael and Alarik in the process.

Freya's breath hitched, as it sometimes did when she realised just how close she had come to not having all of this. If she'd let fear overpower her love for Kjell, if she'd given into the darker side of her grief, she would have built barriers that kept the world out and walked her path alone, never knowing the true contentment and peace that came with loving and being loved.

Kjell looked up at that exact moment, his gaze locking onto hers as if he'd sensed the direction of her thoughts. As if to tell her that he never would have let that happen. He had promised to protect her, and had for her whole adult life. He was the soldier of her heart, the warrior of her soul.

He had once told her that he couldn't have stayed a soldier, that he hadn't believed in it any more, and at the time she hadn't been so sure. But Freya had watched as he had negotiated the most appropriate roles for him to assume as consort, with her brother, who clearly had respect for her husband. Over the years they had spent hours in discussions, long into the night sometimes, and Kjell had become a confidant to her brother. Just as Marit's husband had. The three men had formed bonds nearly as close as their wives. Each couple had gone through their own journeys, deep, painful sometimes, but ultimately it was that which formed the glue that held them all together.

Kjell's bear-like growl bellowing out across the lake to the delighted squeals of their children, drew Freya's eyes back to her family and her feet onward. Kjell hadn't lied when he'd said that the view of the lake was breathtaking in the summer. It was a deep sapphire-blue that sparkled as the sun glinted off the ripples of water like the facets of a jewel. The rich emerald-green forest that framed the lake was full of wildlife that the children both loved and respected. Although their life was in Svardia, Freya's role and duty to her country's people a fierce beat in her heart, her true home was here, in the months they were able to gather with family and friends.

A car's horn beeped and the sudden cry of, 'Far! Far!' from a chorus of children's voices announced Brynjar's arrival with his wife Anita. The first time Freya had met Kjell's father she had been struck by the contrast between the joyous and freely affectionate Anita and the conservatively spoken Brynjar. But she would have to have been blind not to see the love contained in that restraint, as if the ferocity of it was so great he needed to hold it back. She had worried that their children might see it as reticence, but they instinctively responded to his quiet, fierce kind of love. It seemed to balance out the effervescent affection from his wife, to an evenness that filled everyone with a sense of calm and love that was utterly unshakeable.

Brynjar and Kjell had used the last five years to transform the building that Kjell had used as a gym into a cabin with accommodation enough for two families. Using as many traditional methods as possible, what had started as a practical necessity had become a labour of love for the two men as they'd provided home and hearth for their families and future generations to come. Throughout, Freya had watched in wonder as the bond between her husband and his father became stronger and stronger with each passing day and year and, although some wounds were deep and would always be there, the healing was powerful enough to soothe that historic hurt.

Freya was still standing in the wildflower meadow when her children ran past her, focused solely on greeting their grandparents—and whatever treats Anita might have brought with her. She couldn't help but laugh as they raced each other to the cabin, Alarik showing all the restraint of an older brother. Looking back to the lake, her breath caught in her lungs to find Kjell, thigh-deep in the water, his hair slicked back, rivulets of water trickling down his firm muscled torso glinting in the sun, and a gleam in his eyes that was pure heat.

He crooked his finger at her, beckoning her to him, and her cheeks blushed under the weight of his gaze. She shook her head, teasing them both, but his raised eyebrow was a taunt and a promise. He would chase her, she knew, to the ends of the earth if needed, and she would never tire of being caught by this man—her husband, her consort, her one true love.

It was as if she were tied to him by an invisible thread that connected their hearts so, no matter how far apart, they always came back to each other. Now he tugged on it, pulling her to him, and she walked straight into the lake and into his arms, uncaring of the summer dress that was plastered to her skin by the water, and marvelled as he pressed kisses to her lips, her neck and her shoulder, that the once always perfect Princess had finally got her forbidden love.

* * * * *

Lost yourself in
Snowbound with His Forbidden Princess?
Don't miss these other Pippa Roscoe stories!

Rumours Behind the Greek's Wedding
Playing the Billionaire's Game
Terms of Their Costa Rican Temptation
From One Night to Desert Queen
The Greek Secret She Carries

Available now!